D0677355

Slick & Shy
A Love Fulfilled

Rae Bae

Rae Bae

DEDICATION

To my parents Sharon & Johnathan.

Rae Bae

Rae Bae

ACKNOWLEDGMENTS

First and foremost, shout out to God because without him none of this would be possible. I'm so thankful for the love of writing and the talent that he has blessed me with.

For my godmother & Prophetess Tonda West, I thank God on a daily for you. Your prayers kept me even when I was struggling to keep myself.
Thank You!

For the people who are always in my corner rooting for me when I feel like giving up, I thank you.

For the people who have purchased every book and have followed along with every short story, you are greatly appreciated.

For the two people I hold dear to my heart, my two daughters, I love you more than words can say.

Prologue

It was a cold, windy night when I snuck out my bedroom window to go see my boyfriend Mase. He lived off campus in an apartment that he shared with three other guys. I wanted to surprise him tonight so I caught a bus to that side of town.

I knock on the apartment door and the smell of weed almost knocks me off my feet.

"Is Mase here?"

"Yeah he should be in his room."

I walk in and ignore all of the people that were in the den drinking beer, smoking weed, and playing the Play Station.

I try to go in Mase's room, but the door was locked. If I didn't know any better, I would think I hear a girl moaning from inside his room. I bang on the door.

"I'M BUSY."

I bang on the door again more frantically this time. I could hear commotion in the room before the door swings open. He's standing there sweaty with just some boxers on while a female was sitting in his bed holding the covers to her chest.

"Shy what are you doing here?"

I just stood there froze unable to think or react. The man

that I lost my virginity to was now screwing someone else. He was giving them what was only meant for me.

"Who the fuck is she Mase?"

"Shut up Tricia," he tells her.

"Fuck you Mase. I'm leaving."

I could feel hot tears running down my cheeks. I was hurt, ashamed, embarrassed, and heartbroken. Silly of me to think a grown ass man would really be in love with my young ass.

I turn and walk back down the hallway and out the front door. Before I could even make it to the parking lot, Mase was running behind me while putting on a shirt.

"SHY… BABY I'M SORRY."

He grabs me by my hand. Without even thinking, I turn around and slap the taste out of his mouth.

"You told me you love me. You told me that I meant something to you. I gave you my virginity Mase."

"I'm sorry."

"Fuck you. Go back in your apartment and lay up with Tricia. I'm going home."

"Get in the car. You are not about to walk at this time of night. I'll take you home."

"I hate you. I'd rather get kidnapped than to be in the same car as your stupid ass."

"Shy, I know I fucked up. I'm sorry baby."

"You're not sorry that you did what you did. You're just sorry that I caught you. How could you? I thought we had something special."

He pulls me close to him and lifts my head up.

"We do have something special. I love you."

"No you don't."

He leans down and kisses me on the lips. I try breaking away, but he just pulls me closer to him.

"Come on and let me take you home."

I was quiet the entire ride back to my house. I was just hoping my parents didn't wake up and realize that I had snuck out. Instead of him turning down my street, he went in a different direction towards the park.

"Mase, take me home."

"I just want us to talk. I don't want you going home mad at me."

He parks the car and shuts off the engine. He lifts up the arm rest and pulls me over to him. He puts his hand up my shirt while kissing on my neck.

"Mase, I don't want to do this."

"Babe don't be mad at me please."

"Why would you lay up with that girl?"

"I was stupid. I should have known better."

He continues to suck on my neck while lifting up my shirt.

"You still love me?"

I nod my head. His lips soon find mine and we share a wet passionate kiss. He lay me back on the seat and climb on top of me.

And just like that, I forgave him.

It was the first time I found out about Mase cheating on me and it damn sure wouldn't be the last.

Five years later...................

Shy

The clock reads 12:05 AM when I feel Mase slide out of bed. Thinking he was only going to use the bathroom or downstairs to grab a bottle of water, I roll over and fall right back asleep.

When I wake up again it was 3 AM. I had to pee something serious from this baby sitting on my bladder. I look over my shoulder to see the space in the bed next to me was still empty.

After emptying my bladder, I go downstairs in search of my husband. I was a wild sleeper these days so I thought maybe he was downstairs in the den on the couch. I search all over the bottom floor and he was nowhere to be found. His keys were even missing from the place I had last saw them.

Using the Find Friends app on my phone, I trace his iPhone's location. I see that he is across town on Haynes Ave. I throw on my Winnie the Pooh gown and my beige UGG boots. I grab the keys to my Honda Accord and I leave the house in search of my husband.

***

I arrive at a small brick house and see his black Yukon parked in the driveway. I grab my bat out of the backseat before jumping out of the car.

My heart is racing a thousand miles per hour as I bang on the door with my fist. After a few moments, I hear footsteps coming towards the door.

"Who the hell is it at this time of the fucking morning?" A female voice asks from on the other side of the door.

"Shy," I respond.

"Who?"

She opens the door just enough to see who I was. I use all my strength to push the door open even further causing her to fall on the floor as it swung open.

"MASE! MASE!" I scream as I walk in the front door and down the hallway.

Mase walks out of the room rubbing his eyes and buttoning up his shirt. We lock eyes before I start swinging at him with my bat.

"Baby I'm sorry!"

I was not in the mood to hear his bullshit apologies anymore. I struck him across his shoulder with the bat. He reaches out to try and take it from me but I swung even harder.

"I just got released from the fuckin hospital not even 24 hours ago and you laid up with another bitch MASE."

"Baby please just let me explain," he pleads.

He bear hugs me so that I am unable to move.

"Please Shy. Just let me explain. I swear this is the last time."

"Who the fuck is this MASE?" the female works up the courage to ask.

"Did you even tell her you were married? Huh?"

I try to break out of his grip so he pushes me up against the wall.

"I said I was sorry baby. I'm sorry. I had a weak moment. Just please forgive me."

I was sick and tired of hearing the words *I'm sorry* from his dog ass. Nigga had been cheating on me since I was 15 years old. I'm now 20 and aint a damn thing changed. If only I had listened to my parents when they told me he was a dog ass a nigga.

Now look at me, a 21 year old pregnant newlywed to a dog ass nigga. Silly me to think a ring was going to change something.

Mase has cheated on me so many times that I just stopped counting.

He place a kiss on my lips as tears trickle down my cheeks. I push him off of me before taking off my wedding band and throwing it on the floor.

"I'm done Mase."

***

For the past few nights, I had been staying at a hotel. I didn't want to go back to the house because I knew Mase would be there trying to talk his way back into my life again.

I had no idea what my next move was going to be, but I sure as hell couldn't stay in this hotel forever. Mase was making all of the money while I stay at home and take online college courses. Everything was in his name; the house, both cars, and the bank accounts. It was only a matter of time before he put a hold on his credit card that I was using.

I have not spoken to my parents in six months so I was reluctant to call them and tell them how my marriage had already begun to fail. Oh they would just love that!

Having no one else to depend on, I put my pride to the side and pick up my cell phone. I scroll through my contacts until I stumble across my mother's number. I take a deep breath and press send.

After it rung five times with no answer, I just end the call.

"Well so much for that," I say to myself.

I grab some clothes and head for the bathroom to take a long hot shower. Just as I set my clothes on the sink, my cell phone rings. I go back in the room and grab it off of the bed.

I see it was my mom calling back.

I press the answer button but I don't say anything.

"Hello," I hear her say on the other end.

I try to speak, but no words come out.

"Hello," she says again.

"Mama, it's me."

There was a long pause between us. I couldn't hold it in anymore and I begin to cry hysterically.

"Come home Shy. Please just come home."

I could hear in her voice that she was beginning to cry as well.

"We're not mad at you Shy. We just want you to come home."

***

I was only on the third step when the front door swung open. My mom ran out onto the porch to bombard me with hugs and kisses.

"Thank you Lord for bringing my daughter back home."

She rubs my round belly.

"And you're pregnant?"

I shake my head yes. She pulls me into her warm embrace as I cry on her shoulder.

"Everything is going to be alright. You're home now. We got you."

I had been missing my mother so much. A mother's love is EVERYTHING!

"Come on let's go inside," she tells me.

She grabs my hand and I follow her into the house and then to the kitchen. My dad was standing over the stove cooking. He looks up and sees me and my growing stomach.

I walk up to him and give him the biggest hug ever.

"We're glad to have you back home."

I take a seat at the table with my mother.

"So how have you been?" she questions.

"I'm ok."

"You still look so beautiful. I'm just so glad to have you back. Your grandfather is going to want to see you too. You know that right?"

"Yes, I know."

"So what are you having?"

"A little boy."

"You hear that Derrick? We are having a grandson."

"Don't you try and spoil him either Rissa."

"Oh you hush. You already know he is going to be a grandma's baby."

"What are you cooking Dad?"

"Your favorite, stuffed bell peppers."

"I tried to make them once and I failed miserably. Nobody can make em like you Dad."

Slick

"What you got up for today?" one of my partners question as we both clock out of work.

"Nigga, I'm going home to my girl. The same thing you need to be doing."

"Ahh you a sucker."

"Na, I'm about to go home and get sucked on," I say laughing.

"Everybody going to Mase's crib Saturday to watch the game. You down?"

"You know I have to check in with my girl."

"You an old pussy ass nigga."

"Fuck you."

I press the unlock button on my black Ford F-150 Raptor and jump into the driver's seat.

I arrive home to find the apartment looking exactly how I had left it this morning. Clothes were thrown everywhere, the trash was overflowing, dishes were piled up in the sink, and Chanel's ass was still lying around in her pajamas.

"Damn, you didn't even attempt to get out of bed today did you?"

"Well hey to you too. How was your day?"

"Not as easy as yours I see."

I roll my eyes as I sit on the edge of the bed and take off my work boots.

Chanel comes up behind and me and wraps her arms around my neck.

"So I've been looking online for me another car."

"You must got some car money?" I question.

"Come on babe. You know I need a car. I get tired of sitting at home while you're at work. It's boring."

"You're not bored enough for you to get up and go apply for a job I see."

She blows her breath and moves away from me. I get up and go in the bathroom to turn on the shower water. While I was getting undressed, she walks into the bathroom.

"Babe, the car is only four thousand"

"I don't care if it was just a stack. I'm not doing it. Nobody told you to get drunk and wreck the last one. You won't even clean up and have me a hot meal on the table when I get off work, but you expect me to buy you a car. Call and ask your mama hell."

She stomps out of the bathroom.

***

When I met Chanel three years ago, she was a totally different person. She was out celebrating at Applebee's with a few of her home girls and we hit it off. She had just got accepted into the nursing program at a nearby college. Within a few months of us dating, she moved in with me and I bought her a new car to help with her commute back and forth to school and work. Everything was going great or so I thought.

After about a year and a half of us dating, Chanel had managed to flunk out of school, get fired from her job, and total out her car.

It's been about a year and she still has no job, no car, and no desire to get back in school. All she did was sit her ass in the house all day and do absolutely nothing. I mean NOTHING. I had to found out from one of her friends that five months ago she had snuck off and gotten an abortion without my knowledge. When I confronted her about it, she flipped out saying she wasn't ready to be a parent and it's her body so therefore it was her decision. I've always wanted kids so that really hurt me.

I love Chanel, but damn this relationship shit is getting old.

I walk back into the room with a towel around my waist. She was no longer in the room so I throw on some basketball shorts and a tank top before going into the kitchen to raid the fridge.

My keys were missing off the counter and Chanel was nowhere to be found.

I go back into the bedroom and grab my cell phone and dial her number.

"I hope you're out getting us something to eat for dinner since you just jumped in my truck without telling me."

"I'm headed to the mall."

"So you're too tired to clean up, but you got just enough energy to dip out to the mall."

"Damn Slick calm down."

"How you get some money to go to the mall anyway?"

"I borrowed your card babe, but I promise I'm going to pay you back. I need an outfit for Tasty Tuesdays at The Rose tonight."

I end the call before I say something I will regret.

***

While Chanel was out shaking her ass in somebody's club, I was in the bed just flipping back and forth between different porn sites. It had been a week since we had last fucked and I had some pressure built up.

I glance over at the clock as I hear the front door open.

"Have fun?"

"Don't you start? My heart is pounding right now."

"I wonder what pills you done took."

"Fuck you Slick."

She sits on the edge of the bed and unfastens her heels. She slides out of her dress and climbs on top of me.

"I got work in a few hours. Go to sleep."

"I'm horny. Fuck me," she demands as she kisses on my neck.

"Do you know what time it is?"

"Yeah time for you to take this pussy."

She slides her wet, warm pussy down on my dick. My mind was saying no, but my dick was saying YES. I flip her over and place both of her legs in the air as I give her slow, long, deep strokes.

"Go deeper baby…."

I try to murder her pussy. The harder I pump, the more she moans out in excitement.

"Yes Daddy… Go faster Nathan."

Hearing her call me another man's name made my dick go limp. I pull out and look at her.

"Why the fuck you stop? I was just about to get mine."

"WHO THE FUCK IS NATHAN?"

"What are you talking about?"

"Chanel, don't play dumb with me? Who is he?"

"Slick, you're tripping."

She pushes me out of the way and gets out of bed. She grabs her vibrator out of the top drawer and walks into the bathroom. I get out of bed and follow her.

"So you're just going to play me like I'm stupid. Who the fuck is Nathan?"

"You will turn anything into an argument. I can't even catch a good nut without you going off the deep end."

I push her up against the wall.

"After all I do for you, this is the thanks I get."

"Fuck you. You complain about doing shit a man is supposed to do. So what you go to work and pay bills?"

"Well since you know so much about what a man is supposed to do, please enlighten me on your duties as a woman. You don't do shit but sit in this nasty ass apartment all day running up the power bill. Your stupid ass laid up and got an abortion and didn't even have the decency to tell me."

"You mad because I chose to get rid of a child that was growing in my stomach. You are stupid. I'm not ready to be a mother and you can't make me carry your damn child."

She pushes me out of the way and walks back into the bedroom. I follow her.

"I'm sick of hearing about this gah damn abortion. Get the fuck over it already."

"Most men would've been dropped your stupid, ungrateful ass."

"Well I'm not begging you to stay."

"Fuck you Chanel. I want to see how long Nathan puts up with your ass."

Shy

It has been a few days since I last saw Mase because I was still staying at my parents' house. I was lying across the bed scrolling through old pictures of us in my gallery. I was missing him like crazy. After spending damn near six years of our life together, it was hard to just forget about the love we once shared.

I wanted to call him so bad, but I just couldn't bring myself to press send. Not only was he my husband, but he had grown to be my best friend.

Tears roll down my cheek and hit the screen of my phone just as it vibrates in my hand.

At first I was reluctant to answer, but a part of me wanted to hear his voice so bad.

"Baby I miss you. I'm sorry," he announces.

"You don't mean that Mase."

"Yes I do. You know I don't like being without you. Come home."

"I can't."

"Where are you Shy?"

"Mase, you don't respect me as your wife nor as the mother of your child. I need you the most during this stressful time and you're not there for me."

"I promise I'm going to do better. Just please come home."

"I can't. I can't do this with you anymore."

"I've given you enough space. You need to come home now before I come find you. You're pregnant with no money. You do not need to be on the streets."

I begin to cry.

"Baby, I can fix it. Let me fix it ok. Just come home Shy. I miss you. I'm nothing without you. I know I've made a mess of things, but I promise to get it right this time."

It didn't take much persuading for me to sneak out of my parents' back door and head back over to the house I shared with my husband.

He grabs my stuff out of the car and follows me back inside the house. Once we were in the room, I could tell that he was a hot mess as well. His breath reeked of alcohol and his clothes smelt like marijuana.

"I love you," he tells me."

"I love you too."

***

He was lying flat on his back with a mouth full of my pussy as I held onto the headboard. He was eating all of my anger away. After the third nut, I didn't even remember why I was mad in the first place.

I slide down off his face and lay in the empty space beside him.

"Who said I was finished?"

"What you tryna do? Eat it all. You gotta save some for tomorrow."

I walk into the bathroom and turn on the shower. Before I could step inside, he comes up behind me and kisses me on the neck.

"I promise I'm going to do better Shy."

"Actions speak louder than words, Mase."

"I know and that's why I'm going to show you."

"Yeah ok."

He cuffs one of my butt cheeks in his hand.

"Go lay on the bed. I'm not finished with you."

I do exactly as he says. I go in the room and lay down on the bed. He gets in between my legs and kisses from my ankles up to my shaved pussy.

"Daddy been missing you Kitty. You can't leave Daddy starving like that no more."

He kiss on my lips repeatedly.

"You've been bad a very bad girl. Daddy has to make you pay."

He reaches under the covers and grabs my vibrator. He turns it on the fastest speed and places it on my clit while he slides his tongue in and out of my vagina.

"Mase."

"Na, don't try to fight it. It's your fault. You took Kitty away from me. It's time we get reacquainted."

The harder my legs shake, the more he munches on my bag of goodies. I grab a hold of his head and push it down as I feel myself about to explode. I want him to swallow everything he had put me though.

After a few more swirls of his tongue, he comes up. His face is covered in my juices. I watch him lick his lips.

"Was it good?"

"Delicious."

I get off the bed and follow him back into the bathroom once again.

***

Mase and I were lying in bed together watching Double Jeopardy.

"I bet your parents were glad to see you come home. You know they never did like me."

"Don't you start that Mase. You just need to be a man and have a sit down with both of my parents."

"Why the hell would I do that? I'm not married to them."

"Because it's the right thing to do. At the end of the day, they are my family too. It's stressful feeling like I have to choose between my husband and my parents. I want them to be able to come over for Sunday dinners and football Saturdays too."

"Well I'm not kissing their ass Shy. I tried to be cordial to them once before."

"Well how would you feel if your daughter was in love with a man who constantly neglected her and cheated with other women."

"I'm not that guy anymore."

"Ok so show me that by putting forth the effort to establish a better relationship with my parents. I'm their only daughter and it's hard being away from them like this."

"Ok."

"Since you're off today, let's go to the beach. I don't want to be cooped up in this house all weekend."

"Now you know it's Saturday which means the guys are coming over to watch the game around 4."

"If only I could get as much as time as your boys and these hoes in the street."

"Come on now Shy let's just have a good day today."

I get out of the bed to go pee.

"You gone cook the food for the game right?"

"Hell, I wasn't planning on it. Shit, I need a break too."

"A break from what? Your ass don't work."

"You're such a jack ass. Being pregnant is a job all by itself."

"I'm sorry. Baby, please cook something for the game."

"Yeah whatever," I say from on the other side of the wall.

Shy

Mase, his close friends, and a few of his co-workers were in the den watching football on the 60 inch flat screen while I was in the kitchen cooking. I had on rotel, buffalo chicken dip, meatballs, hot wings, and fried wings.

I was standing over the crock pot stirring the meatballs while singing "What's Love" by Ashanti as it blasted from my Bluetooth speaker.

I hear someone laughing. I turn around and come face to face with one of Mase's co-workers, who I had only saw a hand full of times before. He was tall, chocolate, and sexy as hell. I had to put my eyes back in my head considering the fact that I was married, freshly married at that.

"You can sing can't ya?"

"Ha ha ha very funny," I respond.

He just stands there smiling.

"You're almost ready to pop I see?"

"Hell yeah only 10 more weeks to go and our little prince will be in my arms."

"You might not make it that long considering how you're wobbling around."

"Oh you got jokes?"

"Na, it's cute though."

"It's cute and all to you, but painful as fuck to us women."

"Mase is a lucky man. I can't wait till I can experience these moments."

I begin to blush. Mase's voice snaps me out of my day dream.

"DAMN SLICK WHERE YOU AT WITH THE BEER?"

"Calm down lil nigga. I'm on the way."

I watch him open the fridge and grab a case of Budweiser.

"Well it was nice talking to you."

He flashes me a smile showing off his straight pearly white grill before he heads back into the den.

"Damn, he's fine," I say out loud.

Within half an hour, all of the food was done. I fix Mase his plate first and take it to him in the den.

"Here you go babe."

"Thank you, but you're in front of the TV."

"TOUCH DOWN TEXAS LONG HORNS!" one of the fellas yell.

"Damn Shy you made me miss it. Go get me a can soda out of the fridge. What am I supposed to drink with my food?"

"Yall boys better go fix yall something to eat. It ain't gone fix itself," Mase adds.

I roll my eyes and walk back in the kitchen. All of the boys rush in behind me.

"Wash your hands first," I demand.

"I wish my girlfriend would at least attempt to cook for me. It'll be a miracle if she boils some water," says Slick.

"You men sure do know how to pick em."

"Well dang just tell it like it is."

We both laugh. Everybody fixes their food and go back in the den except Slick.

"You can go ahead and fix yours. I know you must be starving right now. These other knuckleheads don't have any manners."

"Thank you. I appreciate that."

I could feel his eyes on me as I fix my plate.

"DAMN SHY. WHERE IS MY DRINK?"

"I'm coming Mase."

I grab a Sprite out of the fridge and make my way back into the den. I hand him his soda and take a seat next to him with my plate in my lap.

"What are you doing?"

"I'm about to eat. What does it look like I'm doing?"

"Not in here you ain't. Do you see any women in here?"

Everybody got quiet and all eyes were on me. I grab my plate and walk out of the den just as Slick was heading out of the kitchen. We lock eyes for a moment and I quickly turn away.

I sit down at the kitchen table and begin to eat alone as my eyes become cloudy with tears.

Slick

I woke up to the smell of food cooking. I roll out of bed, go take my morning piss, and then walk in the kitchen.

To my surprise, Chanel was standing over the stove butt ass naked in nothing but an apron and some black pumps. She now had my dick's full attention.

"Good morning handsome."

I lean up against the wall as she fixes up two plates of food for the both of us.

"What has gotten into you?"

"I've been thinking about what you said and I really do need to step up and appreciate what I have at home," she says with a smile.

"What is it that you want?"

I don't want nothing more than t to apologize for the way I've been acting and how I've been taking you for granted."

She walks over to me and drops down to her knees. Before I could protest, she takes my dick into her mouth.

"I love Daddy Dick."

She kisses from the head of my dick down to my balls.

"I'm sorry for the way I've been neglecting my duties Daddy."

"Show me just how sorry you are."

Within a few seconds, she had swallowed all of my dick and I was enjoying every moment of it. She slow stroked my head with her tongue. It drove me insane.

"You gone be a good girl from now on?" I ask as I run my hand through her hair.

I could feel the sound of her voice vibrating on my dick as she tries to answer me.

"I don't be wanting to fuss at you Chanel. I just want you to do better. We're supposed to be a team."

I grab her ponytail and force her head all the way down on the dick. I could feel my semen releasing and sliding down her throat. She still keeps sucking even after I nut. That drives me crazy. I push her away.

She gets up and runs to the sink to spit out the remainder of what was left in her mouth.

"I done told you about nutting in my mouth."

I come up behind her and bend her over as I ram my already lubricated dick inside her pussy.

"You just hush and take this dick."

"Babe…"

"Na.. don't cry now. This what you been wanting right?"

I grab the back of her neck and ram my big black dick in and out at a fast pace.

"Cum for Daddy, Chanel. Cum on this big dick."

"FUCK ME SLICK!"

"You like it?"

"YES BABY! I LOVE IT."

"This pussy so wet girl."

I smack her on the ass.

"SHITTTTTT CHANEL."

"DO NOT FUCKIN NUT IN ME SLICK."

I pull out and nut on her butt cheeks.

"SHIT GIRL."

***

Chanel and I were laying across the sectional watching Hardball and eating snacks.

"I hate you gotta go back to work tomorrow. I miss when we used to chill like this."

"We are going to get it back like it used to be," I say.

"I know."

"Where my card at? I need to go online and pay my car insurance before I forget."

"It's in your truck in the console."

"Ok. I'll be right back."

I put on my Nike slides and go outside to my truck. I grab my card and just as I was about to close the door, I hear Chanel's cell phone ringing.

I get back into the truck and see her phone on the passenger's side floor board. I grab it and see it was a couple of missed call and missed texts notifications.

The first message that caught my eye on the notification bar was from N and it said *Is your nigga going to be gone again today?*

I slam the truck door and walk back up the stairs to my apartment. I walk inside and slam the door so hard that one of the pictures on the wall fell.

"DAMN WHAT IS UP WITH YOU?" she ask as she sits up from a lying position.

"YOU BE HAVING THIS NIGGA IN MY HOUSE WHEN I AIN'T HERE?"

She jumps up off the couch.

"SO ALL THAT MESS YOU WAS TALKING THIS MORNING WAS SOME STRAIGHT BULLSHIT?"

"Slick, baby let me explain."

"EXPLAIN WHAT. THE FACT THAT YOU A HOE? I SAW THE FUCKIN TEXT CHANEL."

I hold up her cell phone and her eyes got big.

"Slickkk... I."

"GET YOUR SHIT AND GET THE FUCK OUT!"

"Just let me explain. It was nothing like that I sware."

"OK WHATS THE LOCK CODE TO YOUR PHONE SO WE CAN CALL THIS NATHAN GUY TOGETHER AND SEE HOW MUCH OF NOTHING IT REALLY WAS."

She just stands there.

"WHAT'S THE FUCKIN LOCK CODE CHANEL."

"SLICK BABY I'M SORRY."

"WHAT'S THE FUCKIN CODE?"

She goes mute again.

"GET YOUR SHIT AND GET THE FUCK OUT!"

"Where am I supposed to go?"

"OH NOW YOU CAN TALK? I DON'T GIVE A FUCK WHERE YOU GO. GO LAY UP AT NATHAN'S SPOT."

"YOU REALLY GONE PUT ME OUT WITH NO WHERE TO GO?"

"DOES IT LOOK LIKE I'M FUCKING PLAYING WITH YOU? NOW EITHER YOU CAN GO GET YOUR SHIT OR I CAN THROW IT OUTSIDE. YOUR CHOICE."

I sit down on the couch as she storms off to the bedroom to pack her stuff.

"AIN'T NO NEED IN YOU CRYING NOW. YOU WASN'T CRYING WHEN YOU WAS CHEATING."

I wish I had been left Chanel alone. She was the first girl I ever lived with so I really was trying to make it work for the sake of not wanting to start over, but enough is enough. I wanted her ass out of my apartment. She was nothing but a bill and a headache.

There was a knock on the door as Chanel comes out of the back rooming carrying suitcases. I open the door to see her mom standing there.

"May I come in?"

"Mrs. Susie if you're here to try and persuade me to stay with your daughter, it's not going to work. Enough is enough. I pay these bills up in here by myself so shouldn't no other nigga be parlaying in here while I'm at work. Your daughter is foul and I'm tired of talking to her. Let her move back in with you and run up your bills, dirty up your house, and eat up all your groceries."

"Mama let's just go," she says.

I open the door wider allowing Chanel to walk outside with all of her stuff.

"I'll be back to get the rest of my stuff."

"You got ample amount of time to get it now because after today, I'm changing the locks."

"So you really gone talk to me like this in front of my mother?"

I let out a faint laugh.

"I'll sit the rest of your stuff outside before I go to work in the morning," I say before closing the door in her face.

Shy

I was out at Walmart getting some groceries and I just couldn't stop myself from going to look at more baby stuff for Mason.

As I was walking down the aisle, I see Slick pushing his buggy headed towards me.

"Grocery shopping huh?" I say.

"Yeah, I gotta have something to eat for lunch all week."

"Shouldn't your girlfriend be handling all of that?"

"I mean she would if I had one."

"I thought…"

"We broke up," he answers before I could finish my statement.

"Sorry to hear that."

"It's not your fault she cheated on me."

"Honey I've been there plenty of times."

"It's hard to believe a beautiful woman like yourself has been cheated on."

I drop my head down as I blush.

"So what are you doing in Walmart by yourself?"

"Well you know Mase is not about to do anything for himself. Plus, it gives me time to myself and away from the house. I'm supposed to be on bedrest for the remainder of this pregnancy, but I couldn't bear to be in that house another minute."

"It can't be that bad."

"You try living with Mase."

We both laugh.

"Well I'm not going to hold you. Be safe going home."

"I will. Same to you."

I take one last look at him as he walks off. Gah damn he was just so charming.

I grab a few things for Mason before heading back to the house.

***

Mase and I were sitting in bed watching Power while he massages my swollen feet.

"Babe, when are you going to paint the walls in Mason's

room?"

"He's not coming for another 10 weeks. I got plenty of time to handle that."

"The doctor said he can come at any given moment now so you need to go ahead and not wait to the last minute."

"It's not like he's going to be in his room anyway. He's going to be in bed right up under you."

"Whatever you just better paint my baby's room."

"I'll get the boys to come over and help me with it next weekend ok."

"And when are you going to take me to the beach? You promised me we would go."

"You are supposed to be on bedrest yet you're trying to do everything and go everywhere. Just chill babe. We have plenty of time to take trips after Mason is born."

My cell phone rings and it was my mom calling. I haven't spoken to her since I left their house and came back to Mase.

"Hey Ma."

"Hey baby. How are you?"

"I'm good. I'm just sitting in bed while Mase massages my feet. They are super swollen right now."

"Soak them in some Epsom salt and keep them elevated when you are sitting or lying down."

"Ok I will."

"How is everything going?"

"It's good. I went and got some more baby stuff today."

"What all do you need? Your dad and I want to get some stuff too?"

"Well we can never have too many diapers. Yall can get whatever I guess. He's going to be spending time over your house as well."

Mase slides out of bed and walks out of the room. I hear him go downstairs.

"Is Mase treating you right?"

"Yes, everything is going good now. He's been getting better."

"We would like to see you tomorrow if that's ok with you."

"Ok I'll come by while Mase is at work."

"Alright I love you sweetheart."

"I love you more Ma."

We end our conversation. I remove Mase's phone from the charger and connect it to mine. The screen of his phone lit up and I see he had several missed calls and texts from an unknown number.

This muthafucka had his phone on Do Not Disturb cause I sure as hell haven't heard any alerts or felt any vibrations.

Being the nosey wife that I am, I call the number back.

"Hello."

"Who is this?"

"Bitch you called this number so who is this?"

"The wife of the man you fuckin, that's who the fuck I am."

She end the call just as Mase walks back in the room.

"Who the fuck is this bitch Mase?"

"What bitch? You're the one holding the phone."

"Don't your ass play stupid with me. I will throw this phone upside your damn head right now."

"It was probably work related. Quit tripping all of the time."

"So why the fuck she called me a bitch then?"

"Look Shy I've been trying to do right, but you're not about to keep accusing me of bullshit."

"So if a nigga call my phone, you're going to be cool with it?"

"Shy calm down."

I pick up one of my Reeboks and throw it at his head.

"I'M FUCKIN PREGNANT MASE. DO YOU NOT COMPREHEND THAT? YOU'RE STEADY STRESSING ME AND YOUR BABY THE FUCK OUT AND YOU DON'T EVEN CARE."

"I've been loving you since I was 19 years old girl. Don't you ever think that I don't give a fuck about you."

"And you've been cheating on my ass since you were 19 too. Thank you for reminding me of how long I've been a fool for your stupid ass. And then my dumb ass married you thinking shit was going to change. I fuckin hate your ass."

"Calm down before you end up back in the fuckin hospital Shy."

"Like you actually give a damn."

"We've put in too many years to just throw it away. I've been doing right by you lately. You know I have."

"Your dumb ass should've been doing right from the

start then we wouldn't be having this conversation."

"I'm going to bed. Stay up and fuss by yourself. Unlike you I got work in the morning."

"You may as well grab your pillow and take your ass into the guest room or in the movie room because you're not laying up next to me tonight."

"I pay these bills up in there."

"Either you take your ass into another room or I'm going back to my parent's."

"Guess I'm sleeping in the other room tonight."

"I guess so muthafucka."

He grabs a pillow off the bed and walks out of the room.

"Why can't you just be faithful Mase?" I question as his back was turned to me.

He stops at the door, but never turning around to face me.

"I love you Shy. I always have and I always will.

***

The next afternoon after submitting a few online assignments and cleaning the house, I jump in my car to head over to my parents. I was just so tired of being in this house by myself.

Soon as I pull out of the driveway, my gas light comes on. So much for Mase making sure my gas tank was on full every couple of days. His ass was getting lazy. He knew I hated pumping my own gas.

I stop by the Mapco on the way to my parents. I grab my wallet and head into the store.

"Dang we just keep running in to each other."

I look up to see Slick standing in line behind me.

"I'm starting to think you're following me sir."

"I would never."

We both laugh.

"Why aren't you at work anyway?"

"You just all up in my business ain't ya?"

I move up in line and pay for my gas. Before I walk out of the door, I turn to look at Slick one last time.

"Well it was nice seeing you again."

"Same to you."

By the time I reached my car and was getting ready to pump my gas, Slick ran up and snatched the pump out of my hand.

"A woman never pumps her own gas."

"Well aren't you a gentlemen."

"I try. So what are you getting into today?"

"About to go kick it with my parents. I get so bored being home alone while Mase works all day."

"Come and have lunch with me."

"What if I say I already ate?"

"Well come and keep me company while I eat."

I look at him and laugh.

"You are very persistent I see."

"It'll be harmless. Just two friends having lunch and enjoying great conversation."

"I guess I can come."

"Great. It's a restaurant called Mugshots right down the street."
After pumping my gas and his, I trail him down the street to the restaurant he had mentioned.

"So how is the married life treating you?"

"It's not what I envisioned AT ALL."

"How long have you been knowing Mase anyway?"

"We've been together ever since I was 15 years old."

"Damn, that's a long time."

"Yeah a long time to be stuck with someone who doesn't appreciate you."

"Why are you still with him then?...... I'm sorry. That's none of my business."

"Things are different. We're married."

"People get divorced every day so don't use that as an excuse."

"Well dang this feels like an intervention not a lunch date."

"So it's a date?" he asks with a smile.

"I think not."

Slick's cell phone starts going off.

"I'm sorry. I gotta take this."

He excuses himself from the table while I continue to eat my juicy cheeseburger and fries. I pull my phone out of my fanny pack to see if I had any missed calls or texts from

Mase. There were no notifications from him, but I see my mom had shot a text.

Your cousin Terrica is here waiting on you.

I send a response.

I'll be there shortly I promise.

Slick returns to the table just as I was putting my phone away.

"I really hate to say this, but I have to leave to go handle some important business."

"It's no biggie. My mom is waiting on me anyway."

"Maybe, we can do it again sometime."

"I doubt that. Mase wouldn't be too thrilled to know I'm out enjoying the company of another man."

"I guess you're right about that."

He pulls out his wallet and place a 50 on the table.

"Enjoy the rest of your lunch. I'll see you around."

Before leaving, he flashes his million dollar smile. I could feel myself beginning to melt from in between my legs.

Slick

I couldn't get Shy off my mind as I head over to the warehouse. She possessed all of the qualities that I wanted in a woman. Too bad she was pregnant and let's not forget married. Married to one of my co-workers at that. I push the thought of her to the back of my mind as I turn off my truck and step out.

"What's up?"

Richard and I dap it up.

"Did you bring what I asked?"

"Don't be questioning me. When have I ever let you down?"

I open the back door of my truck and pull out a black duffle bag. It hit the ground with a thud.

"That last shipment you had was hitting. The streets ate that up. I hope this the same stuff."

"Yep. I got it sent in straight from California."

"Hell yeah."

He goes to his vehicle and grabs a backpack full of money. He throws it to me.

"It's all there."

"Well I'm out. Let me know if you need some more."

"You already know Imma be in touch."

I jump back in my truck and spin off just as fast as I had come. I had to make it to my bank's safety deposit box before they close.

***

I arrive home and Chanel was sitting on my kitchen counter butt ass naked. I was looking around trying to figure out how in the hell she got in here.

"Why are you in my apartment? Didn't I tell you we were over?"

"Slick, I've missed you and I know you've missed me too."

She jumps down off the counter and makes her way over to me.

"Baby, come on. Don't act like that," she says rubbing my face.

I grab her hand.

"Chanel, I'm not going back and forth with you. Put your clothes on so you can go."

"I want to fuck babe."

"It's plenty other niggas you can get some dick from."

"But I want yours. I've been missing it."

The more she was trying to rub on me, the more my dick was jumping in my pants. I just couldn't resist her trifling ass.

"Chanel, seriously."

"Slick, we've put too much time into this relationship to throw it away."

"Chanel, I need you to go."

"Is it someone else Slick? You've moved on already?"

"I don't have to explain myself to you. Come on. Put on your clothes so you can go."

"Just one last time. Please."

"The last time was the last time."

"Why are you playing so hard to get? I can tell you still want me."

She drops down to her knees and reaches for my zipper.

"CHANEL!"

"Chill out and let me take care of you."

Before I could protest any further, she had already swallowed my dick.

The next thing I know we were back in my bed and I was hitting it from the back. I always fell back into her trap with my dumb ass.

Before I nut, I pull out and let it hit the sheets. I get up and walk into the bathroom to turn on the shower.

"I knew you missed me," she announces with a smile.

"Don't flatter yourself."

As much as I wanted to jump in the shower with her still in my bed, I knew better. She was liable to steal my truck or my debit cards and hit the mall like it was nobody's business.

I told her ass to come on and get in the shower with me. I didn't trust this hoe not one bit.

"So what are we doing this weekend?"

"Chanel, we are not back together. This weekend I'm chilling with my boys. I don't know what the hell you're going to be doing."

"I guess I'm going to be with you and your boys."

"You really are delusional."

"I'm just a girl in love."

"It must be with that other nigga cause you sure as hell don't love me."

"Why do you want to start an argument?"

"We fucked. That does not mean we're back together. I didn't even tell your ass to come over here."

"You wasn't saying that when you were deep in my pussy."

"Of course I wasn't going to say that. It was free pussy."

"Fuck you Slick."

She gets out of the shower. I turn the shower water off and follow suit. I grab my fluffy black towel and wrap it around my waist.

I walk back into the bedroom as she was drying off and getting dressed.

"You're going to miss me when I'm gone."

"Miss what? You don't cook or clean so what exactly will I miss?"

She puts on her sandals and storms out of the room. I get excited once I hear the front door slam. I'm glad she was gone.

Shy

I was sitting on the front porch with my mom and my cousin Terrica. I don't know where my dad was, but he damn sure wasn't at the crib.

"I can't wait till your baby shower. It is going to be so dope," Terrica brags.

"Well I'm glad ya'll are deciding to host it. I just didn't feel like dealing with the stress of trying to put one together."

"How is my little grandson anyway?" my mom asks as she rubs my stomach.

"He is chilling. Do not wake him up."

"How are you and Mase doing?"

"We're good," I lie.

"He could come around you know. He did marry into this family."

"Let Mase stay wherever he's at. I see him enough at home."

"I know that's right. Shit, you need a break too," Terrica explains.

"Why haven't you found a man yet since you know so much?" my mom asks.

"I'm in no rush. I'm just taking my time and enjoying life."

"When you say enjoying life, do you mean you're just having sex with different people?"

I erupt with laughter.

"Mom, you are stupid."

"I'm just saying. I know the kids these days be calling it "living their best life" when we called it hoeing back in my day."

"Auntie, I'm not fooling with you."

"Me either. My mama needs help. I'm telling Dad on you. Where is he at anyway?"

"Girl him and your grandfather been out fishing all day. You know how they do when they get together. Neither one of their asses know how to come back home."

"Are you jealous that grandpa loves Dad more than you?" I joke.

"Oh you hush."

My cell phone rings and it was Mase.

"Where the hell you at?"

"Calm the fuck down. How are you doing today? Me, I'm fine."

"Shy, I'm not in the mood. Where you at?"

"Nigga, I'm with my mama. Damn, why are you acting like that?"

"TELL MASE YOU GOT ONE DADDY AND HE AIN'T IT," my mom preaches.

I guess Mase heard what she said.

"I'm not in the mood for your parent's shit today. I was talking to my wife."

"Mase, it's not that big of a deal. What's wrong?"

"You supposed to be on bedrest or have you forgotten that?"

"I'll be home in a little while Mase. We were planning a baby shower for Mason."

"Mason doesn't even need a baby shower. That's just another form of begging. I already got him everything he needs. Our son is good."

"It's my mother's first grandchild, Mase."

"Ok Shy. Whatever."

He ends the call before I could respond. I look at the phone and just place it back in my lap.

"How the hell you put up with that? Couldn't be me."

"Excuse me. Mase is pushing on my bladder."

I get up and go in the house to avoid crying in front of them. I really wasn't in the mood to hear their opinions about my husband or my marriage.

***

I arrive home to find that Mase wasn't even here and he had left his phone on the dresser so I couldn't track his location. He thought he was smart, but I was smarter.

I pick up the phone and dial the number for Onstar.

"Good evening. How are you today ma'am?"

"I am great. Thank you so much for asking. May I get your name and your reason for calling?"

"My name is Shy Martin. My car was stolen earlier from the mall downtown and I'm trying to track it before my husband gets off work. If he finds out I'm dead."

"I can be more than happy to assist you with that, but first I need you to verify a couple of things on the account. Verify the full name of the owner of the car, last four of their social, the address on the account, and the last four of the card number on file used to make payments."

I relay her my information and before long, I had an exact location to where Mase was.

I put the street address into my GPS before heading over to that side of town. I pull up to his exact location which was an apartment complex that was inside a gated community. Lucky for me, the gate was under repair so I drove right on inside.

After driving around for a few minutes, I finally spot Mase's vehicle. It was backed into a parking space. I park far down the lot so that he is unable to see me. I grab my bat out of the backseat and walk up to his SUV. This nigga had a bitch in the car. I knock on the driver's side window.

He looks at me as if he had saw a ghost.

"Open the door Mase."

"Shy."

"OPEN THE FUCKIN DOOR MASE."

"Mase who the hell is that?"

"BITCH, YOU HUSH AND OPEN THIS MUTHAFUCKIN DOOR SO I CAN TELL YOU FACE TO FACE WHO THE FUCK I AM."

"Put the bat down first."

"You got 5 seconds or I'm busting every window out this muthafucka. 5...4...3..."

Once I got to three, I swing the bat at the driver's side window and it shatters. Glass goes everywhere.

"BITCH IS YOU CRAZY!" Mase screams out.

I reach inside the window and unlock the doors.

"WHAT THE FUCK YOU STILL SITTING THERE FOR HOE? YOU NEED TO BE GETTING THE FUCK OUT."

"I'm calling the police," she tells me.

I reach over Mase, who was slumped down in his seat from the glass cutting his arm and hand, and grab her phone out of her hand. I throw it across the gravel.

"BITCH DON'T PLAY WITH ME. NOW GET THE FUCK OUT BEFORE I BEAT YOUR ASS NEXT."

"SHY, WHAT THE FUCK?!"

"MASE, I TOLD YOU TO STOP CHEATING ON ME. IMMA MAKE YOU PAY FOR HOW YOU DID ME MASE."

I start swinging my bat. I don't even know what happens after that. My anger gets the best of me and I black out.

When I finally came to, I was in the driveway of our house still sitting in the car. I was crying hysterically. I had glass in my hair and blood all over my hands. I was having contractions in my back and Mason was kicking the fuck out of me.

I didn't get married just to get a divorce. I didn't spend six years of my life with someone just to call it quits, but ENOUGH was ENOUGH. I've been through so much with this man and I was tired. Marriage and pregnancy are supposed to be a time of happiness and celebration. Instead, I was going through hell. This isn't love and I know this isn't what love is supposed to feel like.

I hear police sirens. I look in my rearview mirror and see flashing blue and red lights closing in on me.

"FUCK!"

Shy

I had been sitting in a holding cell for the past few hours with nothing to eat or drink. I was hungry. Mason was hungry and he was kicking the shit out of me letting me know that he was ready to eat. My back was in excruciating pain. My feet were swollen and every muscle in my body was sore. I just wanted an Epsom salt bath with a lavender bath bomb. Is that too much to ask for?

"God, I know you're probably not listening, but please do not let me go into premature labor. And please do not let me have my baby in a holding cell."

I hope Mason wasn't dead. He was still the love of my life and the father of my child.

The cell door opens. I look up to see a female officer standing there.

"Come on. You're getting released. This is not a place for a pregnant person to be."

My God was I happy to see her.

"Your parents just posted your bail."

I didn't even get a chance to call and tell them I had been arrested. However they found out, I was thankful. I was just ready to fuckin go.

I walk out into the front lobby and I fall off into my

mother's arms sobbing like a baby. My father rubbed my back.

"Everything is going to be ok," he assures me.

If I had listened to them when they told my stupid ass to leave Mase alone, I would not be in this predicament.

***

I was fresh out of the tub sitting downstairs eating a bowl of cabbages and corn bread. I pour some more hot sauce over my food.

"That's enough damn hot sauce. You don't supposed to be eating hot stuff while you're pregnant no way," my mom fusses.

"But it's so good."

"So good my ass."

"Leave her alone Rissa."

"She already got my grandbaby stressed out. She don't need to be feeding him that hot food. She gone mess around and have hemorrhoids."

"Ma, I'm eating."

"You know your grandfather is disappointed right?"

"Yeah, I know. I'm disappointed in myself. How did yall

know I was in jail anyway?"

"One of the officers knows your father and he gave us a courtesy call. Thank God he did or your ass would've still been sitting there looking pitiful."

"I'm glad I didn't go into labor while I was in there."

"You need to go to the doctor tomorrow to check on everything. The doctor said bedrest and you out here acting like he ain't said nothing."

"Well I gotta go handle some business. Don't let nothing else happen while I'm gone."

My father kisses my forehead. He and my mother share a long kiss before he grabs his keys and leaves out of the back door.

"So tell me what happened."

"I caught him cheating again. I just got tired of it, Ma. I know I was a good woman to him. It's only so much I can take."

"Trust me, I understand. Your father cheated on me once."

"Ma, why are you telling me this?"

"I'm just saying. I know how it feels to be hurt."

"So why did you chose to stick with Dad if he cheated?"

"No one is perfect Shy. After I put my foot down and told him it was either me or them, he did a complete 360 and we ended up getting married. Now look at us. We've been married 18 years and it just keeps getting better. The moral of the story is one day you will find a man who will be all about you and he will change all of his faults to become a better man for you. Just be patient. Time means nothing. I know you've been with Mase since you were a teenager. I couldn't stand his ass then either, but I had to let you learn on your own. I can't save you from everything baby."

"I'm not going back to him. Not this time. It's not even worth it anymore."

"You damn right it's not. You're back at home right where you need to be."

"What if I go to jail for this Ma?"

"Your father and your grandfather will handle it. We will get a lawyer if we have too."

"Thanks Ma."

"You're my only child. I'll go to the end of the Earth for you. Now come on let's go in the den and watch a movie."

We both get up from the kitchen table and make our way into the den.

Slick

I was out at the bar with my boys Rob and Jaylen, Mase, and a few other co- workers. After everything I'd been through with Chanel's crazy ass, a boy's night full of laughter and drinks was much needed. Plus Mase had been out of work for the past two days because something that had happened between him and Shy. I was itching to find out what it was. Her beautiful ass had been on my mind heavy for the past few days.

"So tell us what happened bruh."

"Man, Shy tried to kill my ass and then she fucked up my baby. Yall know I love my truck."

"What did you do this time?" someone asks.

"How you know it was me?"

"Cause you're a man."

We all laugh.

"She pulled up on me when I had some girl in my truck."

"Nigga you must be stupid. How many times has she caught you and you still be doing the same thing? You suck at cheating," Rob explains.

"Well I got a solution. Just don't cheat. That'll solve

everything," I say.

"Oh you shut your sucker ass up. Everybody can't be you, Slick. You probably been at home crying over Chanel these past few nights."

"Screw you Rob."

"You know Rob a hoe too. He can't relate to us real men," Jaylen says.

"Yeah real pussies. Yall some simps."

"Fuck that. Cheating is played out. I'm just trying to love on one woman. All of that lying and sneaking around ain't my style. We're grown now."

"So where Shy at? Did she get arrested?"

"Hell yeah she got arrested. She fucked up my truck."

"Nigga, you had your pregnant wife arrested?"

"What was I supposed to do?"

"Let me take a wild guess…. Apologize for cheating on her and try to make it work. Hell you got full coverage on your truck. Pay the deductible and get it fixed. If you gone grown man things, you gotta be prepared for the consequences. Your wife is pregnant. How the hell did you think she was going to react?"

"Will all the married men please stand up?…. Oh there is

only one and that's me. I'm not taking advice from yall. Marriage is different than being in a relationship. Shit is stressful."

"Don't start that bullshit now."

"Yall don't know my wife like I do. She is crazy."

"Nigga all women are crazy so that's no surprise."

"You had a good wife though man. It's a lot of men out here dying to find a woman like yours."

"Well she's at her parent's house. If they want her, she is not too hard to find," he says in a joking manner.

"You real live crazy man."

"I can't wait till court. I'm going to petition that I get full custody of my son. She's crazy and she's unpredictable."

"You can't be serious right now."

"I'm so serious."

"You're so petty."

"Na, she petty for messing up my vehicle. She better bring me the keys to that Honda too or I'm going to go and get it myself."

"Yall will be right back together so I aint stunt nothing

that you're talking about."

"Well for now I'm teaching her ass a lesson."

"She need to teach you one on how to keep your dick in your pants."

"Oh so now you got jokes? Fuck you."

"I need another round of shots to deal with yall muthafuckas," I say.

"HEY MISS LADY. WE NEED SOME MORE BEERS OVER HERE," Rob announces.

"You're so embarrassing. How does Desiree deal with you?"

"Same thing I'm trying to figure out."

We all laugh again.

***

I leave the bar and on my way home, I stop by the gas station because I had to piss like a muthafucka. On my way back out the door, I see Shy getting into her car. I run over and stop her.

"Damn I just keep running into you don't I?"

"What got you out this time of night?"

"I need to be asking you that Mr. Slick."

"Well if you must know I'm just now coming from the bar."

"You shouldn't be out driving if you've been drinking."

"So you're my mother now? Are you going to give me a spanking too?"

Her smile got bigger.

"Well I'm going to follow you home just to make sure you get in the house safely."

"Ok."

I get back in my truck and she trails me to my apartment complex. Once I get home, she pulls in beside me and rolls her passenger side window down.

"Ok now go in the house and make sure you don't go anywhere else."

"Yes Mama. Do you want to come tuck me in too?" I question flirtatiously.

"Go to bed Slick."

"I will if you come with me."

I lean my head into the passenger's side of her car.

"I got something I want to tell you."

"What is it?"

"Step out of the car."

"Really?"

"I'm not gone bite I promise."

She gets out of the car and we go and sit on the steps leading upstairs to my apartment.

"So what happened with you and Mase?"

"Well I'm pretty sure he done told everybody at work."

"Yeah, but I wanted to hear it from you. It's always two sides to every story."

"After we had lunch the other day, I went to my parents' house. He actually called me fussing because I wasn't at home when he got there. I leave and go home and he's not even there, but I knew he was up to no good because he left his phone at home so I couldn't track his location."

"You can track a location from a cell phone."

"Hell yeah. That's how his stupid ass always get caught. I guess he finally figured it out. So I called the Onstar company and reported his vehicle stolen so that they could give me the location."

"Women are smart as fuck."

"Hell yeah when you got nothing but time on your hands, you have no choice but to figure certain shit out. So I pull up on his stupid ass and he got a bitch in his passenger seat. That's what really set me off. You married but you got bitches in your shit. He so stupid. I was trying to kill his stupid ass for wasting all of these years of my life."

"Na, trust me you don't want no body on your hands. It sounds good, but you aint that type of person."

"And how do you know what type of person I am?"

"Because I can read people."

"Well how come you didn't read your ex-girlfriend?"

I laugh a little bit.

"Oh, you got jokes?"

"I'm just saying."

"You're beautiful you know that."

She turns her head away so I couldn't see her blushing.

"I got a confession to make."
"Ok go ahead."

"I got a crush on you."

"Well thank you I guess."

"So what's up with you and your ex? Are yall finally done this time?"

"Well I'm done with her, but I don't know if she's done with me."

"That's code for yall still fuckin right?"

"Dang why you do me like that?"

"I'm just saying," she laughs.

"So you never told me why you were out at this hour. You should be in the bed."

"I saw that Mase wasn't at home so I went by the house to grab a few of my clothes before he came back. I didn't want any confrontation."

"Yeah I understand that. You don't need to get in any more trouble with your pretty self."

"I like it when you get drunk."

"Maybe I should get drunk and let you follow me home more often."

"Or you can just get drunk at home so you don't have to drink and drive."

"I kinda like the first idea better."

We both smile at each other.

"Well I have to go Mr. Slick. My parents probably going crazy blowing up my phone."

"Can I text you some time?"

"What's your number? I'll text you."

"Don't be getting my hopes up."

"Negro what's your number?"

"Why I gotta be all that baby?"

She gets up and walks to the car to get her phone out.

"So are you going to give it to me?"

"Hell yeah I'll give it to ya. Just come upstairs to my apartment first. I don't want the neighbors to see."

"I can't take you serious right now."

"It's 713-767-8453."

"Ok. I got it Sir."

I walk down the steps over to her side of the car and watch her get inside.

"Text me and let me know you made it safely."

"So you're my Daddy now?"

"Damn I'm Daddy and I haven't even put it on you yet."

"I'll text you once I make it home Mr."

"Ok good night beautiful."

"Good night."

I watch her back out of the driveway and pull off.

My dick was standing at attention. I couldn't wait to get a piece of that. Once I got it, I promise I was going to take good care of it.

I walk in my apartment and close the door before stripping naked and jumping in the bed.

I doze off soon as my head hits the pillow.

Shy

Two weeks had passed since I almost killed Mase's trifling ass. He was a straight bitch for a husband. He hadn't called to make sure his son was ok after what happened or to see how I was doing. Goes to show what type of man he really is. He had even pressed charges on me for assault with a deadly weapon and destruction of property. A grown ass man pressing charges on his wife. What a BITCH!

Last night I had texted him informing him that I would be coming over to move my stuff out of the house and that I would be filing for an annulment of our marriage.

I pull up in the driveway with my parents following behind me in a U-haul that they had rented.

I use my key to walk into the house to see some of my stuff already packed in boxes in the foyer. This was such a dick move. I hated his ass.

He comes to the top of the stairs and just looks at me.

"Why did you just throw my stuff in the boxes like this Mase? You can't just put heels on top of each other. That's how they get scuff marks," I say as I peek inside one of the boxes.

"Did you come here to argue or did you come here to get your stuff?"

"I'm not even about to do this with you today Mase. Yall can start putting the boxes in the Uhaul. I'm going upstairs to see if any of my more stuff is left in the closets and to pack up Mason's stuff."

I go upstairs into our bedroom. I walk inside of the closet and Mase follows me.

He comes up behind me and grabs me by my waist and rubs my stomach.

"You really gone take my family away from me like that?"

"Mase, please don't start acting like you care. You haven't wrote me for two weeks. You didn't know whether I was alive or dead. Hell you didn't even ask how Mason was doing after all of the stress you've had me under."

"What the hell do you have to be stressed about Shy? I take care of you. All you do is take online classes and lay in bed with your feet propped up all day."

"So you don't remember cheating on me all of those times?"

"So what? We've all made mistakes. No one is perfect. Don't act you've never cheated one me."

"Hell I haven't. You took my virginity Mase. You've been the only man I kissed and the only man I've made love too. Can you say the same about me? Hell fuckin no," I say as I broke away from his embrace.

"Tell me what you want from me."

"At this point, absolutely nothing. I'm filing for an annulment on Monday morning."

"Under what pretenses."

"Our marriage was a sham. You've been cheating since we've got married and I have proof. I was tricked into thinking you were someone that you weren't."

"You can't get an annulment Shy."

"According to my grandfather, the Mayor, yes I can. We haven't even been married for a year and if I can't get it annulled, I'll just file for a divorce. How about that?"

"So you just gone walk away that easily?"

"Yep," I respond as I stuff some items inside of my LV suitcase.

"I love you."

"Save that bullshit. You should've been loving me when you were out riding around with bitches in your passenger's seat."

"We weren't riding around."

"Ok smart ass."

I walk pass him out of the closet and out of the room as my mother was coming up the stairs.

"You can take this outside as well Ma."

"I guess you're happy now. You finally got what you've always wanted and that's to see your daughter and I break up."

"This is not what I wanted."

"Yeah I bet. You haven't liked me since your daughter and I first started dating."

"You met her when she was 15 and you were 19. What parent is going to be happy about an over age man trying to manipulate their daughter?"

"Manipulate? She was the one pursuing me as I recall."

"She was 15. You should've known better. What man preys on an innocent girl and then makes her turn her back on her own family?"

"So I did that? You pushed her away every chance you got. Don't blame me for yall family dysfunction."

"Mase, don't talk to my mom like that."

"She started with me Shy. This is the reason why we don't work. Your family always in your damn business."

"Maybe if you treated her better. We wouldn't have to

be all up in her damn business. You know what? I'm not about to argue with you. I'm too damn grown."

"Well act like it then," Mase tells her.

"You talking big boy shit. Just wait till I tell her father. Keep that same energy. Aint that what the young folks saying now?"

I couldn't help but laugh.

"Ma, I'm just about to go pack up Mason's room. I'll meet you outside."

"You're not taking anything out of that room. I paid for everything in there. Hell he's still my son too. Just because we don't work out does not mean I don't get to be a parent."

"Let him have that shit. Just come on Shy."

"And leave my keys to that Honda outside. Since you're so damn through with me and this marriage, quit driving around in a car that I pay the note and insurance on."

"You are such a bastard," my mom says.

"Hey this is between my wife and I. I didn't take vows with you."

"You didn't take vows with Lashondra, Keila, Peaches, and the rest of them hoes either, but you were including them in our marriage. How do you think your son is going to feel when he finds out how you treated his mother throughout her pregnancy?"

"The same way he's going to feel when he finds out you tried to kill his father I guess."

"Same ol Mase. Playing the victim to situations he created."

I throw my keys and my wedding bands at his ass.

"Fuck you Mase. I can't wait to get my damn last name back."

"The feeling is mutual."

I follow my mom back down the stairs and out the front door.

"I HATE HIS ASS!"

Slick

I haven't talked to Shy nor seen her in passing in about two weeks now. Her sexy ass was on my mind all day every day. It was just something about her ass that had me mesmerized.

I was on my way home from work tired as shit. I didn't feel like cooking so I stop by *Juicy Seafood* and get me a to-go plate of crab legs and shrimp with corn and sausage and an egg. The aroma of the food had me racing to the house so that I could strip naked and devour this deliciousness.

I walk in my apartment to rose petals leading from the front door to the bedroom. I hear Avant coming from the Bluetooth speakers. I put my plate on the counter along with my keys and walk in the direction of my room.

I see Chanel in my bed in a red negligee and some black heels surrounded by rose petals.

"How the fuck did you get in my apartment?"

"Does it matter?"

"Hell fuckin yeah it matters."

"I've been missing you Slick. I've been texting you and you haven't been responding."

"Chanel…"

She gets off the bed and grabs my hand. She leads me into the bathroom where I see she had a bubble bath ran for me and everything.

"I'm ready to treat you like the king that you are, Slick."

As usual, my dick had a mind of its own. It was on rock hard looking at all that ass poking out of the negligee she was wearing. She undresses me and we both get in the tub together.

"I still love you babe," she says as she kisses on my neck while straddling my lap.

I had about two weeks of pressure built up and I was ready to release it.

"Chanel, you know you can't keep popping up at my place like this. We're not together."

"I know we're not together, but we're working on it babe. Right?"

"Wrong."

"We've put in too much time to throw it all away Slick. I still love you and I know you still love me too," she explains as she is steady planting kisses all over my neck.

I'm just about to fuck this bitch real good like the last time and send her on her way. Wasn't no getting back together. She better go run game on her other dude because I wasn't falling for it anymore. She wasn't looking for love. Her ass was looking for help.

She slides down on my dick as I held onto her waist. I take her breast into my mouth and twirl my tongue around her nipple.

Maxwell's *Lifetime* was now playing.

She moans into my ear.

"I know you missed me baby," she says.

I hold her down on my chest as my dick explores every inch of her vagina.

"So show me how much you've missed me," I reply.

"Please forgive me Slick. I'm sorry. I just want to come back home."

We get out of the tub and I pick her up and carry her to the room while I'm still beating down her guts.

"SLICKKKKK."

"You like it don't you?"

"FUCK YEAH! I LOVE IT!"

I lay her on the edge of the bed and she wrap her legs around my waist.

"I've been missing this dick like crazy."

"You have?"

"Hell yeah!"

I beat her pussy up as if I was a boxer. This is what her ass been wanting so I was about to give it to her. I feel her about to cum all over my dick.

"SHIT I LOVE YOU SLICK!"

"I love you too Shy."

Chanel pushes me off of her just as I cum all on the carpet.

"FUCK YOU SLICK!"

"You just did and it was good. I might add."

I walk into the bathroom and turn on the shower.

***

I get out the shower and notice it was quiet as hell in my room. I wrap a towel around my waist and go in the bedroom to see if Chanel had taken anything with her thieving ass. She was nowhere to be found so I walk out of the bedroom and see Chanel and Shy standing by the front door. Chanel didn't have on anything but a belly shirt with her ass and pussy all out.

"Apparently I came at a bad time," Shy tells me.

"So this must be Shy," Chanel says with a slick grin.

"And she's pregnant too. Damn, Slick you were talking hella shit about me cheating, but it looks like you've been busy yourself."

"Oh no. We've never slept together."

"Yeah hoe like I believe that lie. He wasn't moaning your name in the bedroom for nothing. I'm done with you Slick. You really aint shit."

She turns and walks away. I could see the sadness in Shy's eyes. She doesn't say anything. She just walks back out the door.

"BITCH WHY THE FUCK DID YOU DO THAT?" I question as I walk back into the bedroom.

"FUCK YOU SLICK. YOU ACT LIKE YOU SUCH A GOOD MAN BUT GOT A WHOLE BABY ON THE WAY!"

"That's not my baby you ass, but what the fuck does that even have to do with you. We're not even together."

"Yeah, but you damn sho been fuckin me like we were still together."

"Because you keep popping up in my damn apartment.

You know what I'm changing the locks. Just get the fuck out Chanel."

"GLADLY! YOU FUCKIN HYPOCRITE!"

She gets dressed and walks out of my bedroom. I follow her to the front door and turn both locks once the door closes.

"FUCK MAN! FUCK FUCK FUCK!"

Chanel ass will fuck up a wet dream if she could. I hear her on the other side of the door still going off.

"WHEN THAT HOE MILKS YOU FOR EVEYRTHING YOU GOT PLEASE DON'T COME CRAWLING BACK TO ME!"

I grab my plate of cold food and a beer out of the fridge and walk back into my bedroom.

"THAT STUPID ASS BITCH MAN!"

Shy

It was Saturday and I just knew today was going to be a spectacular day because it was the day of my baby shower. I haven't had a get together with my family in a long time and it was way overdue. I was just so excited to see everyone today and be surrounded by people that actually loved me.

This past Wednesday I had stopped by Slick's to drop him off an invitation to my baby shower, but I got more than I bargained for. His nappy headed ex was there walking around with her ass out and he was just standing there looking clueless in a towel. He was fine as shit though I can't lie. He had muscles out this world and I saw his dick print bulging through the towel. I still managed to leave an invite on his windshield. I doubt he'd show up though.

My cousin Terrica was doing my make up while my Dad and his homeboys set up everything outside. Mama, Grandma, and Aunt Lorraine were downstairs preparing the food.

"So how has everything been these past couple of weeks?"

"Stressful to say the least, but I'm over it now. I'm just focusing on having a healthy and handsome baby boy."

"He's going to be so spoiled. I can see Aunt Rissa now."

"Girllllll… and when he gets spoiled I'm making sure he

is with her ass so she can listen to him whine and cry."

"How many kids you having after this?"

"Girl zero. The fuck?"

She starts laughing.

"Have you and Mase talked any?"

"Fuck no. He's just so disrespectful. I have absolutely no words for him. NONE."

"Do you still love him?"

"Of course. We were together six years. It's not like I can just turn this shit off when I feel like it. But I deserve better so it's time we part ways."

"Shit everybody can't be like your parents married for 18 years."

"In today's society, you are absolutely right. Nobody knows how to be faithful anymore. Just want to lay up and spread STDs."

"And we ain't got time for that."

"Absolutely not."
She starts taking the flexi rods out of my hair.

"So when are you going to start dating? You've been single forever."

"Aint no man about to tie me the fuck down. I'm only 20. I'm just trying to lie and live."

I start laughing.

"I aint never heard that before. Bitch you stupid as fuck!"

"I'm just saying."

***

I was dressed in a yellow mermaid style maternity dress that hung off my shoulders while wearing some gold sandals and gold earrings. My dad had the back yard decorated so nicely. The theme was Rugrats. The gift table was overflowing with gifts. Mason was truly blessed and I could not wait for his arrival.

After playing a few games and reminiscing on old times, we all sit down to eat.

"Who is that fine hunk of chocolate?" someone asks.

I turn around and see Slick walking out onto the back porch holding a big box that had a picture of a Mickie Mouse stroller and car seat on the front. I smile as I watch him come down the stairs and over to the table where I was sitting.

"Girl he is fine as fuck. God knew exactly what he was doing when he made him," one of my cousins blurt out.

I couldn't do nothing but laugh. I stand up to greet him with a hug.

"So you're not going to introduce me to my future husband."

"Slick these are my crazy ass cousins," I say.

"Hello everyone."

"Do you even know how fine you are? Like do you look in the mirror and be like damn God created an angel?"

He was just standing there smiling from ear to ear.

"Can I talk to you for a moment Shy?"

"Sure. I'll be back guys."

We walk around to the front of the house.

"I appreciate you for coming and for the gift."

"I almost didn't come. I didn't want to be the only male at a babyshower."

"You must didn't see my dad and his friends? This was an opportunity for him to bring out the cooler and the beers."

"You look very nice today."

"Thank you. So how have you been doing?"

"I've been good. I really wanted to apologize to you about what happened the other day."

"No need to apologize. I'm glad you and your girlfriend could work out your differences and make up."

"We did not make up."

"Oh so you had make up sex, but you didn't make up. Oh ok sounds about right."

"Why you gotta be so sarcastic lil lady?"

"I'm not mad or anything Slick. I mean how can I be? You're a single man and I'm a married, but separated woman."

"How come you never text me though?"

"Because I don't need that type of negative energy in my life right now."

"Dang just shoot me down."

"I'm just joking, but I've just been reevaluating my life for these past few weeks. I don't want to ruin anyone's else day by my negative vibes you know."

"You can always talk to me if you're going through something. I thought we were friends."

"Oh so we're friends now? Last time you told me I was your mama."

"I said that."

"Yeah you kinda did."

I look at him and laugh.

He stops walking and looks at me.

"So can I get a text tonight?"

"Maybe."

I look at him and smile.

"So truth moment. You've been on my mind everyday nonstop. I swear it's just something about you girl."

"Would it be wrong of me if I say I felt the same?"

He lean in to kiss me just as I heard my mother calling my name from the front door.

"SHY…. COME ON SO WE CAN OPEN THE GIFTS AND CUT THE CAKE."

"I guess that's my cue."

"Call me tonight so I can hear your voice."

"Ok."

I watch him walk to his truck before I return to the backyard. All eyes were on me.

"What?"

"So you mean to tell me you've been stuck on Mase's stupid ass when you had a man that fine on the side."

"Girl that is not my man in no shape, form, or fashion."

"Well hell hook me up with him then since you're not claiming him."

"He's not mine to claim."

"I gotta start coming around more often so I can see what other fine ass friends you got in hiding."

"That's what I'm saying."

***

I was in the kitchen standing around the bar helping wrap up the leftovers.

"So who was that guy that stopped by earlier?" my mom questions.

"He was just a friend."

"Seems like he likes you."

I begin to blush.

"He's just a sweet guy. It's nothing like that."

"I don't know who you think you're fooling girl. A mother always knows."

"Well we're not hunching if that's what you're getting at."

"Girl that didn't even cross my mind and I hope you not hunching on somebody new with my grandbaby in your stomach."

"Maaaaa."

"I'm just saying."

"I do not want to hear about my daughter having sex. Yall could've saved this conversation for a day I was out or sleep."

"Derrick your daughter is grown and pregnant. I just know you don't think she got knocked up by artificial insemination."

I shake my head and laugh.

"Ma you really are something else."

"Shy, I love you. I just want you to know that. I'm proud to be your mother."

"Don't start that sentimental stuff right now."

"I'm just saying."

She comes over and kisses me on the cheek.

"You're going to be a great mother."

"Thank you."

"Now back to what I was saying. That young man was fine as hell. I wish you could've met him before Mase."

"You're just so petty you know that."

"He looks familiar. Who are his parents?" my dad asks.

"Dad I don't know. We're just friends. I don't even know his last name. We don't even text or talk on the phone. Well at least not yet."

"I peeped how you just threw that in there."
"I'm going upstairs to my room. Yall are too much for Mason and me."

I walk upstairs to my room carrying my bowl of chicken salad and a pack of crackers.

I lay down on the bed and text Slick.

Thanks for stopping by today. It was nice seeing you.

Damn. I finally got a text. I feel like I'm the man of the year right now.

You're just too much. So what are you doing right now?

Laying in bed watching TV wishing I had some company.

Would you like for me to come over and keep you company?

Hell yeah I won't bite.

Only if I could get a foot massage. These babies are swollen.

Of course you can.

Be there in a few.

Ok see you then.

Half an hour later I was pulling into the parking lot of his apartment complex in my mother's BMW. Before I could knock on the door, he opens it with a smile.

"Well damn you must've been waiting by the door?"

"Ha ha very funny."

I walk in and he close the door behind me. I take off my coat as I follow him into the den. He had a cinnamon candle burning which had his house smelling like a piece of candy.

I take a seat on the couch and take off my Ugg boots.

"Yall women and these uggs."

"Don't do me. These are comfortable."

He grabs my feet and place them on his lap.

"So did you enjoy yourself today?"

"Hell yeah. Family means everything to me. We had good food and shared a lot of laughs today. It was much needed after all of the drama I've had going on these past few weeks."

He squirts some lotion in his hand and starts to massage my left foot.

"Well I'm glad everything is getting better for you."

"Thank you. My mom asked about you too. Honey she just swear we got something going on."

"We do."

I look at him and laugh.

"What do we have going on Mr. Slick?"

"A sincere friendship or are we not friends anymore?"

"Yeah we're friends."

"Good cause I was gone have to beat you up."

"So what's been going on in your world?"

"My life is actually going good. For the past few months, I've been repairing my credit because I was trying to get a house built."

"That's whats up. I'm proud of you."

"Yeah my score is actually up to a 710 now because I have two secured credit cards that I pay on time plus my truck note that I pay on time."

"A black man with no kids and good credit. Wow. That's a blessing."

"Monday, I closed on a lot and got everything finalized. So I will be a homeowner soon."

"I'm so happy for you. I love to see black men and women winning. I submitted my last online assignment so I should be graduating with my associates in a few weeks. I'm not going to walk though. I'll just get my shit in the mail."

"Why you don't wanna walk?"

"So my water can break on stage? I'll pass."

He looks at me and laughs.

"So are you and your boo finally done?"

"Hell yeah. I'm through with her crazy ass."

"That's what your mouth says, but your dick says otherwise."

"Don't speak for lil man."

"He's far from little. Trust me I saw the print."

"So you were raping me with your eyes basically?"

"I mean you came out of the room dripping wet with nothing but a towel on. I couldn't help but notice it."

"So you be low key checking a nigga out?"

"Whatever Slick."

"So how many more weeks you got until you finally drop? It looks like your stomach gets bigger by the day."

"I am 32 weeks. As long as I can make it to at least 36, I'll be happy especially with all of the stress I've been under."

"Well I'll be praying for a safe delivery for you and little man."

"Thank you."

While he was still massaging my feet, I somehow dozed off. I woke up to an empty den, but the TV was still on and he had given me a thick blanket. I grab my phone and see it was 3 AM and I had missed a bunch of notifications from my mother.

I get up and walk in Slick's bedroom and see that he is sprawled all over his king sized bed.

I sit on the edge of the bed and shake his shoulder. Half asleep, he jumps up and looks at me.

"Damn you scared me. Is everything ok?"

"I'm about to head home. I didn't even realize I had fallen asleep on you. I must've been tired as hell."

"It's no problem. You sure you gone be alright driving home at this time of morning."

"I'll be fine Daddy Slick."

"Don't say it like that. I might like it."

"Get up so you can lock the door behind me."

"Stay with me until the morning."

"Technically it's already morning. It's a little after 3."

"You know what I mean."

"I hope you don't think I'm about to lay in this bed on the same sheets you been hunching other bitches on."

"You're crazy as hell you know that."

"So I've been told," I say with a laugh.

He gets up, grabs his pillow, and follows me back into the den on the couch.

"I hope you haven't been slobbering on my couch cause you were tapped out good last night."

"I haven't slept that good in a long time."

"Well you're welcome. I have that effect on people."

I look down at him while he lay at the other end of the couch.

"Good night Slick," I reply with a smile.

"It's morning remember," he responds jokingly.

Slick

It was Sunday and I was getting ready to head over to my mother's house for dinner. It had been a few weeks since the last time I saw her or my twin sisters so I had to go and show my face.

Before walking out of the house, my cell phone rings in my pocket. Thinking it was Shy calling, I answer it without looking at the caller id.

"What's up?"

"I need you to meet me again. Same location as the last time," Richard announces.

"I am having Sunday dinner with my mother so you're going to have to wait."

"What time you think you can link?"

"Didn't I say I am having dinner with my mother. You gone have to wait. I'll call you when I'm done."

"Nigga, you are a lousy ass drug supplier."

"Well find another one."

I hang up the phone and continue walking out of my apartment.

***

My mother had a nice three bedroom, two bathroom brick house in a cul-de-sac about twenty minutes away from me. I walk in the house carrying some pink roses that I had picked up along the way. She was in the kitchen standing over the stove.

"Now you supposed to had this finished before I got here," I joke.

"Oh you hush."

She turns around and gives me a hug and a kiss on the cheek.

"These are beautiful," she compliments as she takes the flowers and put them in a vase.

"Where the twins at?"

"In the back. Gone back there and tell them to come in here and set this table for dinner."

"You already know they not about to set no table. Probably don't even know how."

"Don't be talking about my babies."

"You got them spoiled rotten. I wish you would've spoiled me like that."

"Boy gone. You are 25 years old. Let that hurt go."

"One day but not today."
I take a seat on the counter next to the stove.

"Why your shadow not with you? You know she don't let you leave the house by yourself."

"We broke up."

"Thank God for that…. I mean oh no, I'm sorry to hear that. What happened?"

"She cheated."

"Welp, I hate to say I told you so, but I kinda did. I told you she was no good. She just wanted a man to take care of her ass and you fell right in her trap. You need you a woman that got something going for herself and got her own money. Quit letting these women make a fool out of you son."

"Like you said I'm 25 so you should not be all up in my business in terms of relationships. Let's talk about your love life? I rode by one night and saw a Honda outside. Who was that?"

"I'm the parent. I don't care how old you get, your business is my business."

"Ok so whose car was that backed up in the driveway? Don't try to avoid the question."

"I'm grown and for your information, he was just a friend."

"What kind of friend? Friends don't come over at that time of night."

"Do you pay any bills in here?"

"Actually I do. I just paid your light bill and water bill for the past three months since you're no longer working."

"Oh, so you got a problem helping your Mama, but you can take care of these hoes."

"Well you asked did I pay any bills in here. I hope that nigga breaking bread since he laying in between your legs."

"Worry about you. I got me."

She was setting the table as my 14 year old twin sisters, Saniyah and Mariyah, walk into the kitchen. I jump off the counter and greet them both with hugs.

"How have my favorite girls been doing?"

"Good," they respond in unison.

"How are those grades looking? They better be looking damn good since I see yall got the latest iphones in ya hands."

"Well my grades are fine," Saniyah assures me.

"Ok and what about yours?" I ask Mariyah.

"Well I had a D in science, but I think I've pulled it to a

low B or high C."

"What the hell you doing getting a D in the first place? I told Mama she got yall spoiled as hell. Don't even clean up, but got a new damn phone. That's probably where all my money been going."

"Don't you start Slick," Ma tells me.

"You need to quit treating them like babies and give them chores and stuff to do. Every week they at the mall with their friends and she got a dang D. I couldn't even go outside and play if I had less than a B. Kids these days got it made."

"Did you come over here just to fuss cause you could've stayed at home for that?" Mariyah tells me.

"You know how your brother is. It wouldn't be him if he didn't show tough love. He means well. Now let us all sit down and eat. I didn't prepare this delicious smelling food for nothing."

I wash my hands and take a seat at the table. Just as I was about to chow down on my beef tips covered with gravy and rice, I get a notification alert. I pull my phone out of my pocket to see it was a text from Shy.

I enjoyed your company last night. Hope you are having a great day Mr. Slick.

My face lit up with a smile.

I am now thanks to you beautiful. How are you doing?

"UH UH! PUT THAT PHONE AWAY. THIS IS FAMILY TIME. YOU CAN TALK TO THEM LITTLE HOOCHIES LATER."

"How you even know it's a girl?"

"Cause I can see the way you over there cheesing like a chess cat. Dang let your mama get at least a couple hours of your time. You know you don't stop by but once a month, if that much."

I put my phone back in my pocket.

"Who was that anyway?" she questions.

"Get you some business," I say jokingly.

Throughout the entire dinner, I was all smiles. I just couldn't get Shy off my mind. Just being around her made me the happiest man alive, but I knew I couldn't fall head over heels. Technically she still belonged to somebody else and she was pregnant with his son. However, the idea of being a step father didn't seem to farfetched.

Loving her was just one risk I was willing to take.

Shy

It was a sunny Monday afternoon and my mother and I were sitting outside on the front porch enjoying each other's company. I was rubbing my stomach while my feet were propped up in another chair.

"This dang Mason is giving me hell right now," I say as I tap the side of my stomach in order to persuade him to switch positions.

"Leave my damn grandbaby alone."

"Your grandbaby need to leave me alone."

"You should've thought about that before you laid up."

I look at her and laugh.

"You're so funny you know that."

"I should be a comedian."

"Na just keep being a house wife. Don't embarrass yourself."

"Your father is just so excited to be a Paw Paw. He was up last night looking at your baby pictures and crying."

"Why?"

"We're just so happy you're back home. We've prayed

and prayed for God to give you back to us. Not only did he answer our prayers, but he gave us a grandson. It's a beautiful feeling."

"You gone make me cry."

"You cry all the time anyway."

"No I don't," I say.

"Shy please. You came out the womb crying and haven't stopped yet."

My mom stops talking and looks up. It was Mase's SUV pulling into the driveway.

"What the hell is he doing here?" she questions.

"Your guess is as good as mine."

He steps out the car and walks up onto the porch.

"Hey how are you ladies doing?"

"What you want Mase?" I question before he could even finish his sentence.

"I wanted to talk to you and to check on our son."

"I'll be in the house."

My mom gives him a stank look before getting up and going in the house. He takes her seat and pulls it closer to me before sitting down.

"Why are you here?"

"I've been missing you," he responds as he grabs my hand and kisses it.

I snatch away from him.

"I'm sorry about what has transpired between us these past few weeks."

"You mean past few years."

"I don't want to fuss with you babe. I just want us to be on good terms for our son's sake."

"Mase, you are full of shit."

"You took away my car knowing that was my only means of transportation. How am I supposed to get back and forth to doctor visits after Mason is born?"

"Your parents have three cars Shy. You really think me taking your car is stopping you from getting around?"

"That's not the damn point. You're my husband. I shouldn't have to rely on my parents for anything."

"I apologize. If I give you your car back will you come back home?"

"Hell no Mase. We are done."

"I thought you said you wanted us to be a family and to raise our children under the same roof."

"Well I lied. Go and be a family with all of those different girls you were meeting up with."

"I'm ready to change Shy. I really am."

"It's just a little too late quite honestly."

He places his hand on my stomach.

"He moving like crazy. He must've heard his Daddy's voice. Have you been going to your weekly appointments?"

"Yes I have."

"Is he head down yet?"

"Yep. I doubt I make it to 36 weeks. It'll be a miracle if I do."

"I want to take you out for a picnic tomorrow after work. Would you be down for that?"

"Mase, I have no desire to be around you to try and work on our marriage. I'm over it now. I was stupid to think marrying you was going to make a difference and that you would be committed to me only. You're never going to change."

"There is no guideline on how to be a perfect husband

Shy. We all make mistakes."

"Cheating for 6 years is not a mistake, it's a choice."

"It's not the same without you at home. It's lonely. I have no one to talk to or rub on when I'm in bed. I know I've been taking you for granted, but this shit sucks."

"Mase, you love me but you pressed charges on me. How does that work?"

"You fucked up my truck and you tried to kill me."

"If I wanted to kill you Mase, you'd be dead."

"If I get the charges dropped, will you give me another chance?"

"I'll consider it," I lie.

"That's all I ask. Well I'm about to head on over to the house. Can I get a hug before I leave?"

We both stand up and he pulls me into his arms.

"I miss you so much man."

He tries to kiss me, but I turn my head.

"Call me if you and my son need anything."

"Yeah sure."
I watch him back out of the driveway before going

inside the house. I go upstairs in my room and plop down on the bed.

***

A few hours later while my mom was downstairs cooking dinner, I was upstairs in my room and I was in excruciating pain. I am feeling like my back is about to fall off. I was down on the floor on my knees while leaning over the side of the bed. A sharp pain kept hitting in between my legs. I was just praying I wasn't in labor and these were just Braxton Hicks contractions.

My mom walks in the room and sees me on the floor.

"Girl what the hell is wrong with you."

"I'm hurting," I say as I burst out in tears.

"You mean to tell me your ass been in here hurting all this time and ain't told nobody. Where you hurting at?"

"My vagina is on fire right now and sharp pains keep hitting my back."

"Where your hospital bag at? I'm about to go get your daddy so he can carry you down the stairs. We taking your ass to the hospital. Ass sitting up in the room going into labor and you aint said a damn thing to nobody."

"It's in the closet."

She walks out of the room and goes to get my father and

he walks in with the same attitude.

"Bless your heart. You look like you're in labor. How long have you been like this?"

"For about an hour."

"She stubborn just like your ass Derrick," my mom says.

"Oh hush up Rissa. Ain't nobody tryna hear all that. Grab her hospital bag and go start the car."

My mom does as she's told and my dad picks me up off the floor.

"Today is the day I'm about to be a grand daddy. Don't come right now Mason. Give us about ten minutes to get you to the hospital and in a bed."

"What if he comes in the back seat of your car?"

"Then you owe me a new car," he jokes.

While in route to the hospital, I reach out to Mase to let him know that he needs to be on the way. I really didn't want to look in his face, but I was not about to purposely make him miss the birth of his first child.

"You calling to say you want to come home?"

"Nigga, hell no. I'm calling to tell you I'm in labor and to get your ass to the hospital."

"It's a little too early aint it?"

"Well duh Mase. Stop with all the questions, get your ass out of bed, and come the fuck on."

I hear a female's voice in the background.

"You already chilling with another hoe. See what I'm talking about Mase."

"Shy, it is nothing like that. I'm at the damn gas station."

"I muthafuckin bet. GET YOUR DUMB ASS TO THE HOSPITAL!"

I end the call before he could say another word.

As much as we argue, I already know my son is going to be an exact replica of his stupid ass daddy. That's probably what he wanted anyway.

"Is he coming?" my mom questions.

"He better be hell."

I shoot Slick a text.

I'm headed to the hospital. I'm about to be a mommy.

Shy

I was now sitting up in bed holding a naked baby boy with a head full of hair and hazel eyes to my breast.

"You are just so perfect Mason. I'm going to love you forever and ever."

Mase was standing beside me rubbing his hand up and down Mason's back.

"Thank you for blessing me with a son. I'll always be grateful for that."

"He is just so handsome. I got the best grandson in the whole wide world," my mom brags.

She had her phone out taking all types of pictures and videos.

"He's so tiny. My baby looks like a little rat."

One of the nurses walk in the room.

"Congratulations on your new bundle of joy. Because he's premature, we're going to have to take him to the nursery just to make sure he is as healthy as he is handsome."

"So I'm not going to be able to sleep with him in the

room with me tonight?"

"I'm afraid not, but if all of the tests turn out good he will be back first thing in the morning."

"Mommy's going to miss you Mason."

"I'll carry him to the nursery. I need some bonding time with my first grandson."

"Your first and last," I announce.

"That's what you think."

My mom swaddles him up in his baby blanket before leaving out of the room with the nurse and my dad right behind her. Mase takes a seat on the side of my bed.

"Thank you Shy. Because of you I'm now a father. I will always love you for that."

"And because of you I'm now a mother so I'm appreciative as well."

He tries to sneak a kiss in, but I turn my head to the side.

"You're still mad at me?"

"I'm happy as hell right now true enough, but that still doesn't not change the fact that we are separated."

"I meant what I said this afternoon. I miss your ass man. It's lonely as hell without you around."

"I don't want to talk about that right now. Don't try and spoil a good moment."

I just wanted Mase here for moral support and that's it. I wasn't trying to talk about our relationship and how much he is willing to change. I heard all of that bullshit a million times and I didn't want to hear it anymore."

"What if I say I'll go to marriage counseling. Will that change your mind about everything?"

"At this very moment, I am genuinely happy for the first time in a while. I now have a son who I know for a fact is going to love me unconditionally and I'm never going to have to question it. The only thing that we need to be focusing on at this present time is how we can be great co-parents for our son."

"Despite how you may feel about me, I'm going to show you from this day forward that I can be the husband and father that you need me to be."

"It's a little too late for that honey."

He pulls my wedding bands out of his pocket and places them in my hand.

"I'm not going to sign any papers to have this marriage annulled. I want to work on our union and I know deep down you feel the same. We've put in too much time to let it end like this."

I just look at him without even saying another word. He talking about marriage counseling, but little did he know my mind was on a whole nother man and his name was Slick. I wasn't about to go back to that depressing ass house with him just to get treated good for about a month and then get cheated on again once things were starting to get better.

"Do you want me to stay with you tonight?"

"You have work in the morning so go home and get you some rest."

"I can miss work. My son was just born. They will understand."

"Mase, take your ass home. I'm exhausted and sweaty and I just want to go to sleep."

"Ok, I'll let you get some rest. I'll be back tomorrow ok."

"Ummm hmmm."

"I love you baby."

He kisses me on the forehead before getting up and walking out of the room. I quickly throw the wedding bands on the bedside table. Nigga had lost his mind if he thought I was about to put those rings back on.

I look up at the clock and it is going on 10:00. Just as I was about to doze off, my cell phone rings. I knew it was Slick because of the notification alert that I had assigned to his name.

"Dang, I thought you had forgot about me."

"I could never do that. How are you feeling?"

"Tired and hungry as hell."

"How much did little man weigh?"

"5 pounds and 2 oz."

"Dang he's a tiny little thing."

"I know it."

"Well congratulations beautiful. You're a mother now."

"Thank you. I wish I could see you tonight, but I know you got work in the morning."

"That don't mean nothing. I can always make time for you."

"Isn't that sweet. I feel special."

There was a knock on my room door.

"Hold on someone is at the door," I say into the phone.

"Come in."
In walks Slick carrying some balloons, a teddy bear, and a Chipotle bag.

"Hey gorgeous."

He comes over and gives me a hug and a kiss on the cheek.

"You're just so awesome. I was just about to tell you to bring me something to eat."

He takes a seat next to the bed.

"I just passed your parents as I was getting off the elevator. They said they will be back in the morning and to get you some rest."

"Did you stop by the nursery to see Mason?"

"Yes and he is handsome as ever. Looks just like his daddy."

"Let's just pray that he doesn't act like him."

"Well we better start praying now," he jokes.

"I sure do appreciate you for stopping by."

I catch him glancing at the rings on the bedside table.

"Mase wants to get back together," I blurt out.

"Yeah I peeped that. So what are you going to do?"

"Not a damn thing. Moving back in with him is the

farthest thing from my mind right now. I just want to focus on my son."

"And me."

I look at him and smile.

"So how was your day?"

"Same ol bullshit at work as always, but I just go to do my job and take my ass back home."

"Are you and your ex still hooking up?"

"Na, I told you I was done with her remember."

"You said that the last time yet when I popped up she was there."

"Well as of today, I'm done. Her and I haven't had any type of dealings with one another. You sound like you're low key jealous or something."

"Never that."

"You feeling the kid aint ya? I see you blushing over there."

"Whatever Slick. So what's your real name anyway cause I just know your mama didn't name you that."

"It's Solomon if you must know."

"Solomon. It has a nice ring to it."

"Solomon and Shy... That sounds nice doesn't it?"

"I don't know. Maybe."

"So what are your plans for the summer? You aint pregnant no more so you can live it up."

While I was telling Slick about all the trips I wanted to take with Mason, I notice he had gotten really quiet. I look up and he is sound asleep in the recliner chair.

My heart was so full of joy watching him. Out of all the places he could've been, he decided to be here with me.

I dim the lights in the room using the bed control and soon after, I was dozing off to sleep myself.

Today was a GREAT day.

Slick

I was lying in bed with nothing but a tank top and boxers on while facetiming Shy. Her and Mason were now back at her parents' house. She had just finish burping him and lying him down in the bed.

"So how is the breastfeeding coming along?"

"Breastfeeding is the devil. My breasts are sore as shit. It's so damn time consuming. I have to pump damn near every hour."

"You got this. You will get the hang of it in no time."

"So how have you been?"

"I'm good. I need to be sleep, but I just couldn't get you off my mind."

"The feeling is mutual, but if you need me to let you go I will."

"Na, I want to stay up and see your beautiful smile."

"Slick, I really am falling for you. Even though I am separated, I am still technically married so I don't want to over step my boundaries with you."

"You're not over stepping any boundaries. I can't lie I'm falling for you too. I just don't want to fall and you not be there to catch me."

"I wouldn't string you along if I knew I wasn't feeling you like that. I don't play with people's feelings. I've had mine played with too long."

"Well I assure you I am nothing like Mase. I treat women the same way I would want someone treating my mother. I can't rush you to be with me, but just know that once you and Mase are officially over I'm going to be all over you."

"I can't wait to kiss those sexy lips of yours."

"That can be arranged right now. Just say the word and I'll be on the way."

"I wouldn't make you come all the way over here to see me when I know you have work in the morning."

"You lucky cause I was about to jump outta bed and rush over there."

"Is that so?"

My dick was rock hard just thinking of all the things I could do to her little ass.

"Damn. I'm going to have to talk to you in the morning. Mase is calling to check on Mason."

"Ok. Good night beautiful."

"Good night handsome."

Our video chat ends. I pull up my favorite porn website and beat my dick at the thought of me giving Shy long, deep back strokes. I was feening for her like crazy and I just knew I had to make her mine.

***

The next day at work, the fellas and I were sitting around the picnic table kicking the shit and enjoying our lunch break. Mase walks up and takes a seat across from me.

"So how's fatherhood been treating you?" Tiger asks.

"It's a blessing man. The best feeling in the world honestly."

"So have you and Shy had a chance to hash out yall differences?"

"Things are not one hundred percent back to how they used to be, but we've been talking about her coming back home. It's only right that we raise our son under the same roof and try to work on our marriage."

"Grown man shit right there. Can't do nothing but respect it."

Hearing Shy's name had me on edge. I was a damn fool falling for a married woman thinking she was going to honestly leave her husband. She hadn't even filed for divorce yet and I was already head over heels for her."

"For our one year anniversary, I'm thinking of renewing our vows this time in a church setting in front of both our families."

"Boy, you the only one in the group that's married. Shit, we are getting old."

"Speak for yourself, I'm getting younger," says Rob.

"I'll catch up with yall inside."

I get up from the table and go back inside building.

***

Since I got off work, Shy had been calling and texting nonstop. I wasn't answering. I was just annoyed with her for lying to me. She could've just been straight up and said she wanted to work on her marriage.

I clean the house, put on a load of clothes, and cook me a taco salad for dinner. Before sitting down on the couch to devour this salad, I grab me a cold beer out of the fridge.

I had downed three beers while eating and watching Taken 3 on the Amazon fire stick. My cell phone going off knocked me out of my daze. I answer it.

"Damn, good to know that you're alive. I've called you at least three times."

"Yeah ok."

"What's wrong with you? You don't want to talk to me?"

"Honestly, no."

"Are you drunk Slick?"

"Why do you care? Don't you gotta husband you need to be worried about?"

"What has gotten into you? What changed since last night when we were on Facetime?"

"Ask yourself that question."

"Ok Slick. I see how it is."

"Shy, why are you playing these games with me. Why you act like you care so much for me when you're talking about getting back with your husband?"

"I'm not getting back with my damn husband. If I wanted his ass back, I would not be at my parents' house right now. I don't know what has gotten into you Slick, but lose my number. You playing way too many games right now. If you and your ex wanted to get back together then cool, but don't try and make me look like the guilty party. I've been nothing but honest with you since day one."

"And I haven't?"

"Apparently not Slick, but whatever. You have a great night."

The call ends. For a few minutes I just sit there and look at the screen. I get up, grab my keys, and take off in the direction of her parents crib.

Her mom opens the door while holding Mason who was tightly swaddled in a blanket to her chest.

"Come in," she instructs.

I follow her into the den where Shy's father was sitting on the couch watching Family Feud.

"You can have a seat. We don't bite," he teases.

"By the way, we have not been properly introduced. I'm Derrick and that's LaRissa, but everybody calls her Rissa."

"Well nice to finally get your names. I'm Solomon, but everyone calls me Slick."

"You look very familiar. You sure I don't know you?"

"No sir. I don't think so."

"So you like my daughter?"

"Yes sir I do, but only as a friend."

"You do know she's married right?"

"Yes I'm aware of that. I also know that she's not happy. I just want to be the one to keep a smile on her face you know."

"I'm starting to like this guy. So are you close to your family?" Rissa asks.

"Yes, my mother and I are very close. I have a set of twin sisters who I am close to as well. As a child, I was close to my dad before he passed away."

I hear Shy coming down the stairs.

"Ma, why do you keep coming in my room and getting Mason out of his basinet? He had just went to sleep."

She stop in her tracks when she sees me. She had on a long Mickey Mouse pajama shirt with some yellow footies.

"Slick, why are you here?"

"Because I missed you."

I see her face light up.

"Plus I cooked a taco salad and I brought you some."

"Well your dad and I are going upstairs. Come on little man. You gone sleep in the room with Nana tonight aren't you?"

"It was nice talking to you Slick, but us old folks gotta get some rest," her dad tells me before getting up and following her mom up the stairs.

Shy comes and takes a seat on the opposite end of the sofa.

"Come a little closer. I don't bite."

I pull her next to me.

"I'm upset with you Slick."

"I apologize. I was just acting out because of my emotions. My feelings were hurt."

"Well you hurt my feelings too."

"Can I get a hug?"

She leans in to hug me and I sneak a kiss. She didn't even try to fight it as I slip in some tongue.

"I'm falling for you Shy."

"I've already fallen for you Slick."

She kisses me again.

"I've been waiting a long time for that."

"You want have to wait much longer. I go and file for an annulment through the courts tomorrow."

"Good cause I'm ready to have you all to myself."

Slick

Several weeks had gone by and I was getting to spend more and more time with Shy. Every now and then she would come over at night after putting Mason to bed and we would get to spend a couple of hours together. She was completely different from most women and I liked that about her.

Mason was away with his father and his side of the family for the weekend. I had made plans for us to spend the entire day together.

"Where are we going?" she questions.

"You just sit back and ride lil lady, but it's going to be some place really special."

"This is my song."

She turns the volume up as Jaheim's *Put that Woman First* blasts from the speakers.

"When she starts bringing up old dirt and the fights keep getting worse. Findin numbers in her purse better put that woman first. And you notice she ain't wearing her ring."

"What you know about that youngin?"

"You better take note and put that woman first."

"I do put you first."

"Where are you taking me? It looks like we going into some woods and shit. I hope you're not trying to kill me."

"Why do you have to be so dramatic?"

"Because you like it."

We pull up in an open field and I cut the truck off.

"Come on let's go."

"What in the hell are we doing out here?"

"Just come on miss lady."

I grab the picnic basket and blankets out of the back seat. I grab her hand and lead her through a trail. We came out in an open area that overlooked a waterfall.

"Slick, this is beautiful."

"I knew you would like it."

"And you packed a picnic basket. You're quite the gentlemen aren't you."

"Well I try to be."

Once we were settled in, I pull out two wine glasses from the basket and a bottle of red wine.

"Since you're breastfeeding, I know you can't drink like that. However I did google that you can have at least one glass of red wine and it wouldn't hurt."

"Just what I need."

She was sitting in between my legs leaning back on my chest while sipping out of her glass.

"I appreciate you for doing this. These past seven weeks have been absolutely insane. Being a mother is tiring, but at the same time it's so rewarding."

"I'm glad you get to kick back and relax today. You deserve it beautiful."

"Truth or dare?" she asks.

"Dare."

"I was hoping you were going to say truth, but I dare you to kiss me."

She turns around to face me and I pull her onto my lap for a very passionate embrace.

"I like kissing on you," I admit.

"Well kiss me again."

We share another intimate kiss before I fall back purposely with her on top of me.

"Your lips taste like candy."

"I was thinking. Let's have a sleepover in the den tonight. We can make a pallet on the floor, eat junk food, and watch movies all night."

"I'd love that. As long as I get to rub on that big ol booty tonight."

"You're such a tease guy."

"How?"

"You just are."

"I know you want some of this sexy chocolate, but nah you gone have to wait for it."

She looks at me, laughs, and then kisses me again before sitting up.

***

We were back at my place and while she was in the bathroom soaking in a bubble bath that I had ran for her, I was in the den getting everything set up for our movie night.

I could hear fussing coming from the bathroom so I walk in and see Shy still soaking in the tub fussing on the phone with who I assumed to be Mase.

"Nigga don't call me with that shit like you just father of the muthafuckin year. I did pack enough breast milk. Your dumb ass should've looked in your mama's fridge before calling me. You just wanted to piss me off. Don't call me anymore until it's time for me to meet you with Mason."

She ends the call and throws the phone down on the floor.

"What was that about?"

"Mase stupid ass had the audacity to call going off on me talking about I'm a bad mother. How I was so ready to run the streets that I didn't even pump enough milk for Mason. Unlike him, I'm a full time mother and I know what the fuck to pack before sending my son anywhere. What I look like sending my son off for the weekend without enough milk?"

"Shy, don't let him get to you. He only called because he know you're probably out enjoying yourself and wanted to kill your vibe."

"I'm so over him Slick. He just makes my flesh crawl."

"Well hurry up and get out of the tub. I'm ready to watch a movie and lay up under you."

"Ok, I'll be out in a minute."

I walk out of the bathroom and grab a beer out of the fridge. I hear my cell phone vibrating from on the couch.

Quit ignoring me. We need to talk. I miss you.

It was none other than Chanel. I delete the message and put my phone on Do Not Disturb mode for the rest of the night.

Shy walks in the den wearing nothing but a towel.

"Can you give me something to sleep in? Don't be giving me one of your exes old shirts. And please don't give me no shirt of yours that she has worn."

"You're just so demanding. Give me a kiss first," I say as I stand up in front of her.

She stands on her tippy toes so that she could kiss me and I snatch the towel from around her waist.

"I can't wait till I get to make love to all of this. You really gone be mine then."

I pick her up and place her on the kitchen bar. We begin to kiss. I kiss down to her neck and then to her breasts. I go even further down to her pussy and spread her legs apart. I attack her vagina with wet kisses and flicks of my tongue.

As soon as I start getting into it, I hear banging on the door.

"SLICK I KNOW YOU'RE IN THERE. WE NEED TO TALK SO OPEN UP AND QUIT IGNORING MY MESSAGES!"

It was none other than Chanel. She couldn't have picked a more perfect time.

"Fuck man."

"Yeah you got that right. Gone open the door and see what your little girlfriend want."

I could tell Shy was pissed. She pushes me out the way, gets down off the bar, and storms into my bedroom. Me and this bitch haven't had no type of dealings with each other for at least two months. Now all of a sudden, she wants to pop up.

"SLICK! YOU MUST GOT YOU ANOTHER BITCH IN THERE. I HOPE SHE HEAR MY ASS TOO."

I open the door.

"What Chanel? What?"

"Baby, I miss you and you haven't been returning any of my texts or calls. Like damn what's up?"

"What's up? We broke up months ago. Please don't get amnesia."

Shy walks from the back ground fully clothed.

"So yall still messing around?" she questions.

"THIS THE BITCH THAT YOU LEFT ME FOR SLICK. REALLY THOUGH?"

"Chanel, I'm not about to do this with you. We are done. I made it perfectly clear the last time we fucked that I wasn't going to keep doing this with you. We're done. Let it go and move on. It's been months now."

"Slick, I'm pregnant."

"Oh and?"

"What you mean and?"

"Why the fuck you telling me this Chanel? Clearly it's not mine."

"Well that's my cue to leave. Slick, can you take me home?"

"Chanel, you have a good night. Please don't show up on my doorstep again."

"So you gone turn your back on me and your unborn?"

I slam the door in her face and lock it.

"Can you just take me home Slick?"

"Shy."

"No need to explain. Just take me home please."

"Baby please don't go."

"If you don't want to take me home, I'll call a Lyft."

"Just hear me out. I swear I haven't had no dealings with that girl. If she's pregnant I know for a fact it's not mine.

She's fuckin delusional. She's been texting me daily for weeks and I don't even respond. Please don't let this ruin our night. It was so posed to be all about us."

"I just want to go home. Can you please take me home?"

"Ok sure thing. Let me go put on some clothes."

"Thank you."

The whole ride to her parents was silent except for the sound of Shy sniffing in the passenger's seat. I hated Chanel with a passion for this stunt she had pulled. Out of all the days her dumb ass could've popped up, she chose today.

Fuck it, I was getting me a new number as soon as possible.

"Shy, please don't go to bed mad at me."

Before the truck could stop good, she jumps out with her bag and runs up the front porch. I watch her unlock the door and go inside before pulling off.

Some date night this is turning out to be.

Shy

After that little stunt that happened over the weekend, I have not said a word to Slick. He had been trying to get in touch with me, but I just did not have the time for any more drama on top of what I was already dealing with.

I was sitting in my room breastfeeding Mason while scrolling through the Fashion Nova website. Retail therapy does the body good. I add a rainbow colored romper to my cart just as my mama walks in my room. She takes a seat on the bed next to me.

"He stay eating. That's why he so big now."

"They say babies that are breastfed tend to be bigger than the ones that are on Similac."

"I see. My baby getting juicy. I'm just happy he's gaining weight. He was looking like a squirrel when we first brought him home from the hospital."

"Well my baby ain't a squirrel no more," I say rubbing my fingers through his curls.

"I haven't heard you mention Slick's name lately. How has he been doing?"

"Alright I guess."

"You don't like him anymore?"

"His ex just keeps popping up and stuff. I don't have time for any more drama right now you know."

"So are they still messing around?"

"He said they not, but I don't know. I don't really care. It is what it is. He's a single man so he can do whatever he wants to do."

"I actually liked him. Any man that can get in your father's good graces is alright with me."

"Have you been in contact with Mase?"

"Not really. Every time we talk he wants to start an argument over nothing. I swear he likes getting me upset."

"He just mad because you finally see him for who he really is and that's a snake. I don't care who you end up with as long as it's not him anymore."

"Dang was he that bad?"

"Do you even have to ask?"

We both start laughing.

"I'm so proud of you. You've got one degree under your belt and you're a great mother."

"Sometimes I feel like a failure."

"Why is that?"

"I just never imagined I'd be a 21 year old who is separated from her husband and has a child. I always wanted to be like you and Dad and raise my kids in a two parent household."

"Everybody's story is not going to be written the same. What God had planned for me might not be planned for you honey. You're only 21. You're going to make mistakes. This is the time to make them. I know people in their 30's that still don't have their life figured out. Just because you're not with Mason's father does not mean you want find a man that will love you and your son as his own. Sometimes a step parent will love and care for the child more than the actual parent."

"You're right."

"Be thankful. You have a good support system. You and my grandson are not homeless nor broke. You are in your right mind and you have perfect health. Quit looking at the things in your life that seem to be going wrong and look at what is going right. One day you're going to look back at this moment in your life and see how far you've come and how much you've accomplished."

"Thank you. I needed this talk."

"Anytime. You want Mason to sleep in there with us tonight."

"Na, he's going to sleep in here with his mama. Yall be tryna kidnap my baby."

"I see how it is. You gone be wanting me to keep him one night for you and I'm going to remember this conversation."

"Really Ma? Get out your feelings."

"You know you gotta have me a granddaughter now right?"

"Says who?"

"Says me. Mason is going to want somebody to play with."

"So. Yall left me lonely when I was a child. I had to create imaginary friends. He can do the same."

"Well I'll give you two more years and then we want a granddaughter."

"You can always go adopt."

"I didn't say I wanted a child. Being a grandmother means I can give them back to you after I've already spoiled them rotten."

"And you wonder why the only way Mason will go to sleep is if he's lying on somebody's breast."

"I had nothing to do with that."

"Yeah right," I say.

"Well I'm going to bed. Maybe your father will give me some good sex."

"Good night Ma. Please get out of my room. I did not want to hear that."

"Gul how you think you got here."

"Artificial insemination."

"Na, the same way you got knocked up with Mason."

"The stork dropped him on your doorstep that's how."

"Girl gone somewhere with that."

She kisses Mason on the forehead and leaves out of my room. I burp him and then lay him in his basinet while I go take a hot shower.

***

I was in standing in my bathroom mirror putting on my Aloe Vera facial cleanser. I peep in the room to check on Mason and he is chilling in his swinger sucking on his two fingers while Sesame Street was on.

"You look more and more like your daddy every single day," I say to no one in particular.

Ma storms in my room.

"SHY GET DOWNSTAIRS. YOU HAVE GOT TO

SEE THIS!" she says excitedly.

"What is it?"

"JUST COME ON!"

"Dang. Let me wash this off my face first."

"WELL HURRY UP!"

"I'm coming."

I throw my towel on the bathroom counter and follow her back down the stairs. The living room was full of roses.

"What in the world."

"This is all for you."

"Who sent these?"

"Here's the card," she says handing it to me.

A Pro flower associate walks in carrying more flowers and a big brown teddy bear.

"That's enough. Don't you bring no more flowers in here. Give them out to the neighbors or something. Better yet take them home to your wife or girlfriend. I can't even see my living room floor."

He walks back out the door as I open the card.

How many roses does it take to say I'm sorry? –Slick

My face lit up as the doorbell rings.

"I'll get it. It better not be that man with no more flowers. They gone think somebody died."

Ma walks off as I stood there just smiling as I kept rereading the card. He was so sweet. I was beginning to feel bad for ignoring him these past couple of days.

"So are you ready to answer the question?"

I turn around and see Slick standing there. I give him the biggest hug.

"I don't want to be mad at you."

He kisses my forehead.

"Are you ready to talk now?"

I shake my head yes.

"Derrick, you gone have to take notes. You letting the new generation of men outshine you. You know what this means don't you?"

"What?" my dad questions.

"It's a sign that I need a new car."

"Well I didn't get that sign did you Shy?"

"Welp that's my sign to go upstairs."

I grab Slick's hand and lead him upstairs to my room. I see Mason had fallen back asleep. He closes the bedroom door and kisses me like never before.

"Shy, I'm in love with you," he tells me in between kisses.

"How do you know?"

"Because I've never felt this way about anyone before."

I wrap my arms around his neck and kiss him more intimately. He pulls away.

"We gone be late if we keep at it."

"Late for what?"

"Our flight."

"Flight?"

"Yeah," he says while smiling.

"Pack your bags while I go downstairs and persuade your parents to watch Mason for us."

"Really?"

"Yes Really."

"How should I pack? What are we going to be doing? How is the weather going to be?"

"Shy just pack some clothes."

"Baeeeee."

He picks Mason up out of the swinger and walks out of the room before I could say another word.

***

My very first time riding an airplane and I ended up in Vegas. Boy was I excited. I was like a little kid at Disney World. We check into the Skylofts at MGM Grand and it was absolutely beautiful. It was like a mini apartment.

I was walking around the loft admiring how beautiful it was when Slick grabs my waist and pulls me close to him. He kisses me on the back of my neck.

"You like it?"

"Of course I do. This is absolutely breathtaking and the view of the city is to die for. I can't believe you planned all of this for me. How much did it cost you?"

"Price means nothing to me. I'll pay whatever for you."

"Thank you baby."

"You're welcome. Now go take a shower and change

into something casual."

"You're not going to get in the shower with me."

"If I get in the shower with you, it's gone be trouble so na."

"Well at least come in the bathroom and keep me company."

"You just can't get enough of having me around can you?"

"Well I mean I didn't get to see you for three whole days."

"And who fault was that?"

"Yours babe."

He laughs as he follows me into the bathroom.

"So are we going to the strip club while we're here?" I ask from inside the shower.

"We can do whatever you wanna do babe."

"I'm just so excited. I have never been outside the state of Texas."

"Never?"

"I mean I did when I was a kid when we took trips to see

relatives and stuff. I was young so that doesn't count."

"Well I like to travel so we are going to be everywhere."

"You must be making some good as money at your job honey."

"I make enough."

"Did you mean what you said earlier?"

"When I said I love you?"

"Yeah."

"I wouldn't have said it if I didn't mean it, but my actions are going to tell you more than my words ever will."

"I appreciate you for being such a good friend to me lately. I read this quote somewhere that said if sex was not in the equation, could you really vibe with the person you're with. We haven't even had sex and we actually have a good time when we're together."

"Sex is cool, but shit I want to know if I can chill with you all day and not get tired of your ass. Can we hold an intellectual conversation? Can I vent to you about the stress I may be under? As you get older, sex becomes an option and not a priority. Well at least that's how I feel. I can't speak for the other men out there."

"My mama was asking me about you last night and telling me how much my father likes you. I was mad at you so I wasn't trying to hear it."

"Mama always knows best."

I step out the shower wrapped in a fluffy bath towel. I walk over to him and stand in between his legs.

"Don't be trying to start nothing now Shy."

"I just want a kiss that's all."

He kisses me on the lips.

"Now go get dressed."

"Ok Daddy."

"Keep that same energy when we get back in the room tonight."

I go back into the bedroom. While trying to find something nice to wear, Slick was the only thing on my end. My six weeks been up and I wanted to fuck something. AND BAD!

Slick

After walking the strip and sightseeing for about an hour, we head to the restaurant where I had made a reservation.

Once I tell them my last name, a server comes up and escorts us to a private room. They had us a candle lit table right next to a big glass window. The view of the city was amazing. I pull the chair out from the table and watch Shy take her seat before sitting down across from her. The server hands us our menus and then leaves.

I look up from scanning over the menu and see Shy just staring at me and smiling.

"What?"

"You're just so awesome. I've never experienced anything like this."

"Well this is just the icing of the cake. I have got so much more in store for us these next few days."

"You know the restaurant fancy when they don't have prices listed."

"Price means nothing when you're with me. Order whatever you like."

The server comes back and sits a basket of bread and

butter in the middle of the table.

"Are you both ready to order?"

"Yes, I would like the seafood platter with a rib eye steak cooked all the way. I'd take a bottle of Hennessey Cognac with that."

"For an appetizer can I get a shrimp cocktail and then I'd like the lobster tail. I'll just drink what he's getting, but bring a glass of ice water as well."

He collects the menus and leave out of the room.

"You sure you gone be able to handle what I'm drinking. That's a grown man drink."

"Well if I get too faded, just carry me to the room ok."

"I've never seen you drunk before. This is going to be hilarious."

"Just don't let me make a fool of myself."

"If I see you starting to act crazy, I'll just get the rest of our food to go."

"Good idea."

***

I could tell Shy wasn't a drinker because after just two shots of Cognac, she was a totally different person. She was all over me as we rode the elevator back up to our loft.

"Baby I want to fuck right now," she whines.

She starts trying to undo my belt buckle.

"Babe, I got you. I promise."

"You're not taking your pants off fast enough."

It was a good thing no one was in the elevator but us. I grab her by her waist and pull her to me.

"I'm going to take real good care of you tonight I promise."

She kisses on my neck.

"My pussy is so wet right now."

I pick her up as the elevator doors open and carry her all the way to the room. We walk in to rose petals leading from the door to the bedroom.

Before I could even close the door good, she was already stripping naked. She grabs my hand and leads me to the marble table that was in the dining area.

"I want you to fuck me right here."

She sits on the table and pulls me close to her as she undo my belt while I take off my shirt.

"You sure this is what you want?"

"Yes, I'm sure."

We kiss until I was fully naked. I lay her back on the table and place her legs on my shoulders. I start kissing on her breasts and end up with my face buried deep in her pussy. It was the sweetest. Her moans made me go even harder.

"Yesssss baby yessss. Oh my fuckin God."

She holds my head down and locks her legs together around my neck.

"Yes baby right there. Slickkkkkkk I love you. Ooohh I love you I love you I love you."

I lick, suck, and nibble on every inch of her treasure box. She was going insane as she releases back to back orgasms.

Whoever was watching us through the window was getting one hell of a show. Knowing I probably had people tuned in was just turning me on even more.

"Please don't stop babe. Please don't," she pleads.

She runs her fingers through my waves as I gently suck on her clit.

We make our way from the table to the bedroom. I was still standing when she drop down to her knees and begins to suck my dick. She swallows it without any hesitation.

"DAMN GIRL!"

If Cognac had her acting like this, I was gone buy her plenty of it. I grab her ponytail and fuck her throat. Her mouth was so warm and wet. I was trying everything in my power not to nut quick. I wanted to enjoy every moment of this.

You would think we were making a flick with the performance she was giving.

"If I had known it was gone be like this, I wouldn't have waited so long," I tell her.

"You like it?"

"Like it? Baby I love it."

She wraps her freshly manicured nails around my shaft and begins to stroke it while sucking on the head.

"Man your mouth will drive a nigga crazy girl. I swear I aint letting you go. You my girl now. You hear me?"

I pull my dick out her mouth and slap it against her face.

"You hear me?"

"Yes Slick I'm all yours I promise."

She grabs my dick and shoves it back in her mouth.

"You like Daddy dick don't ya?"

"Umm hmm," she moans.

"You a beast with that mouth girl I swear you will drive a nigga fuckin crazy. I promise you don't never have to worry about me going anywhere. I'm here to stay."

"You better be."

I look down and see her looking up at me while she still had my rock hard dick in her mouth.

"Tell me you love Daddy Dick."

"I… love… it."

I feel myself about to nut. I pull my dick out of her mouth and watch my cum skeet all over her breast.

I bend down and give her a kiss.

"I love you girl."

"I love you too."

***

Shy's screams fill the room as I was filling her guts with nothing but dick.

"Quit running babe. I thought you could take it."

I see tears running down her cheeks.

"You want me to stop?"

"No, keep going."

She was steady trying to get away so I pull her back down and lock my arms in between her legs.

"I don't ever want to let you go."

I lean down and my lips find hers.

"Don't ever turn your back on me," I say in between us kissing.

She wrap her arms around my neck.

"Just show me the same loyalty that I show you and you don't have to worry about me going anywhere."

I grab ahold of the headboard with both hands and start giving her long, deep strokes.

"SLICCCCCCCCCCCCCCCCCCCCCCCKKKKKKKK KKKKKKKKKKKKKKKKKKKKKKKK!!! AHHHHHHHHH!!"

We end up falling on the floor. I instruct her to get on all fours and she abides. I pull her arms behind her back and fuck her like crazy.

"Who pussy this is?"

"Slick, it's all yours."

"Cum for Daddy. I feel you trying to hold it. Let it go. You will feel so much better."

"Babyyyyyyy pleaseeeeee."

"Please what? I'm not gone stop. Imma make sure I please you all night long. This what you want aint it?"

"YESSSSS BABY I WANT IT!"

I feel the warmth of her juices colliding with the lubricant of the condom. I let her arms go and she falls down on her stomach.

"Don't tell me you tapping out."

"I'm not."

I get up.

"Go get a glass of water. You gone need to be hydrated for this next round," I say as I smack her butt cheeks.

Shy

The next afternoon Slick and I have brunch together and then we hit the strip mall to do a little shopping. While he was in the Polo store splurging, I go next door to Osh Kosh in search of Mason some new clothes and shoes.

While trying to decide between two different collar shirts, my phone vibrates from inside my clutch purse. It was none other than my mother.

"Hey Ma."

"You could've at least called us and let us know you had made it safely."

"I'm sorry. I was just so excited to be riding on an airplane for the first time."

"Are you enjoying yourself?"

"Hell yes. Slick got us staying in this nice loft that's like on the 30th floor or something and it overlooks the city. It's so beautiful Ma. I'm gone have to record a video. I have never saw anything like it."

"You deserve a nice getaway. Mase's mother called wanting Mason for a couple of hours so I packed him a bag and sent him with her."

"Oh well that's fine."

"I'm ready for you to come back now. I done got used to you being here every day."

"We will be back sometime Sunday."

"What yall doing now?"

"Shopping. I'm in Osh Kosh looking at Mason some stuff. Slick is next door in the Polo store."

"I can't fool with yall rich folks. Yall too boujie for me."

I laugh a little bit.

"Mama please. I just had a little money put back. You know I don't mind going broke for my baby."

"That's how us mothers are. But I'll let you get back to what you were doing. I guess I'll make your father take me out to the movies or something."

"I love you Ma. Video chat me once Mason makes it back home."

"Alright I love you too."

After getting Mason four outfits and some sandals, Slick and I link back up as he was exiting the Nike store.

"Did you find everything you were looking for?"

"Yes, I got Mason a few items."

I grab his hand and intertwine my fingers with his as we continue walking. This was the happiest I had been in a long time. I was just hoping it wasn't too good to be true.

"I'm really enjoying spending time with you babe. I feel like the luckiest woman in the world right now."

"You are the luckiest woman in the world and the most beautiful woman too."

I stop and look at him.

"Promise me you not gone break my heart."

"I promise I'm not going to break your heart."

He gives me a kiss on the forehead and we continue walking hand in hand.

***

Slick had a fun filled day planned for us. First he had set up for us to go on an ATV tour which was fun as hell I might add. Afterwards we went on a bus tour of the Grand Canyon. On the way back to our hotel, Slick saw the big Ferris wheel and wanted us to ride it together which I thought was super romantic.

We finally make it back to the room a little after 8.

"I really really enjoyed you today. Thank you for all of

this."

Once I shower and put on one of his long white T shirts, I didn't feel like going back out to get dinner so he ordered room service.

We sit in the bed eating cheeseburgers and French fries while watching Home Alone and drinking some type of brown liquor he ordered.

"Slick so tell me about your parents. You think they will like me?"

"Well if my father was still living, I'm pretty sure he would like you. I don't know about my mama. She is very hard to please."

"I'll pass on meeting her then."

He looks at me and laughs.

"I'm just saying babe. I don't want her to not like me."

"Did you and Mase's mother have a good relationship?"

"We never really talked on the phone, but when she was around we were cordial to one another. I guess it was like that considering the fact that my parents hated her son."

"How did yall end up together anyway because he is 26 and you're only 21?"

"I met him when I was 15 and he was 20. I thought he

was my knight in shining armor."

"And your parents were ok with that?"

"Hell no. I didn't tell them about Mase until I was 16, but I was already having sex by then. Plus I lied about his age. I told them he was 18 at the time, but of course they found out that I was lying. By that time it was nothing they could do. I just thought I was the luckiest woman in the world even after the times I caught him cheating. And to think my dumb ass still married him."

"How is the annulment coming along?"

"Oh, it's coming. My grandfather is the mayor so he's talking to his friends in high places trying to get it pushed through as soon as possible."

"Your grandfather is the Mayor? You never told me that."

"I thought I did. It must've slipped my mind."

"So do your parents work?"

"Hell na. My dad got medically discharged from the military so I think he gets a monthly check. My mama ass is just spoiled. She aint worked since I was damn little."

"Well they live in a nice house and drive nice cars so it looks they are doing well for themselves."

He takes our empty plates to the kitchen and when he

returns to the room, I was naked in bed. I open my legs. Using my middle finger, I begin to play with my clitoris while he stands in the door way and watches.

"Come here baby."

He walks over to the bed taking off his shirt and boxers along the way. I bite down on my lips as he climbs on top of me. First kissing me on my lips and then down to my neck and breasts before going further down south.

He use his hands to spread my pussy lips apart. He slides his tongue from the hood of my clit all the way down to my opening. He does this a few times.

"Quit teasing me babe."

He was face down in my pussy smacking on it like candy and I was loving every minute of it. He pulls me down and flips me over so that I am riding his face. He place his arms behind my knees so I can't move.

"You like this sweet pussy don't you?"

He begins to moan letting me know that he was indeed enjoying every minute of it.

"You keep eating this pussy like that and I promise I aint going nowhere. You do it so good baby."

He loosens his left hand from behind my knee and grabs me by the neck. Him choking me only made me moan louder and cum harder.

"FUCKKKKKKKKK SLICKKKKKKK!"

I roll over from on top of him.

"Where you going? I'm not finish."

"Baeee."

"Na this what you wanted right. Come here."

He gets out of bed and picks me up. He has me up against the glass window with my legs around his neck while he was sucking and biting on my pussy.

"Baby what if somebody sees us?"

"So let em see babe. This my pussy."

I run my hand through his waves and down the nape of his neck.

"I love you Slick. God knows I love you."

He carries me from the bedroom to the kitchen still sucking on my pussy along the way.

This nigga was turning me into a straight freak. What happens in Vegas was most definitely going to stay here.

Shy

We arrive back in Texas late that Sunday evening. I was sad that our baecation had come to an end, but I was missing the hell out of Mason.

Slick pulls up in my parent's driveway and I just sit there looking at him for a few moments. He grabs my hand and kisses it.

"I enjoyed you this weekend beautiful."

"The feeling is mutual."

Before I know it, I see Mase's SUV in the rearview mirror.

"FUCK! That's Mase."

"So. What the fuck he supposed to do? You aint gotta be scared. I got you."

Next thing I know Mase is pounding on Slick's window.

"WHY THE FUCK YOU GOT MY WIFE IN YOUR SHIT YOU BITCH ASS NIGGA?"

Slick reaches up under his seat. I'm assuming for his pistol. I grab his hand.

"Babe don't kill him please."

"YOU GONE HAVE TO SEE ME HOMEBOY. YOU POSED TO BE MY MANS BUT YOU SNEAKING AROUND WITH MY BITCH."

At that moment, Slick opens his car door and jumps out. He punches Mase in his shit causing him to stumble backwards.

"Watch your muthafuckin mouth when you talk about her. Learn some damn respect."

"BITCH NIGGA."

Next thing I know they are fist fighting. I didn't know what to do but blow the horn repeatedly to get my parents attention and for them to come outside. I call my ma's cell phone at the same time.

"Is that you outside blowing the damn horn like you're crazy?"

"TELL DAD TO COME OUTSIDE. SLICK AND MASE ARE OUT HERE FIGHTING."

I end the call and jump out the truck to try and break it up.

"STOP IT!"

"YOU FOUL SHY. AFTER ALL WE'VE BEEN THROUGH, YOU GO AND LAY UP WITH THIS PUNK ASS NIGGA. FUCK YOU AND HIM."

"You got two seconds to get the fuck off my property or I'm shooting your ass. This the last time you gone disrespect my daughter. I let you slide too many times because of the fact that she loved your dog ass, but you aint gone disrespect her at my own damn house."

"YOU WRONG SHY AND YOU KNOW IT. YOU CLAIMING TO BE SO DAMN DOWN FOR ME, BUT YOU RIDING WITH MY FUCKIN NIGGA. MAN FUCK YOU."

"FUCK ME MASE. FUCK YOU. YOU CHEATED ON ME SIX YEARS. YOU CHEATED ON ME MY WHOLE DAMN PREGNANCY. NA NIGGA IT'S FUCK YOU WITH YOUR STUPID ASS."

He gives me one last nasty look before getting back inside his vehicle and speeding off. I turn and look at Slick before breaking down into tears. He pulls me to his chest and wraps his arms around me.

"I told you I wasn't going to let anything happen to you. I got you."

He kisses me on the forehead.

"Quit crying now. Ain't nobody gone touch you especially not no pussy ass nigga."

"He was real bold to pull up in this yard with that bullshit. I've been sparing his ass for way too long. His mama would've been picking out a suit if I was out here when he first pulled up."

"Oh I got the pistol in the car. Shy stopped me from grabbing it. I'm not about to play with ya. Imma let these bullets do the talking."

"You got that right. Let's get on in the house before these nosey ass neighbors start calling."

"Gone in the house babe. Me and your daddy gone get your bags."

"Ok."

I pull away from him but not before we share a quick kiss.

***

I was in the room lying in bed with Mason on my chest. He was just staring at me with his big old eyes.

"You missed me didn't you? Yeah I know you missed mama."

My mom walks in the room and sits on the bed.

"So how was Vegas?"

"Oh it was dope. I had such a good time."

"That boy really likes you Shy."

"Yeah I know. I like him too"

"I'm not telling you what to do, but take your time. Love is not going anywhere I promise you."

"I am. Ain't that right Mason?"

"He is spoiled."

"I wonder where he gets that from."

"Not me."

"Yes you and Daddy. I done got hungry again."

"Gul it's going on 10:00. Take your ass to bed."

"Yes ma'am you're the boss. Ma I've been drinking all weekend so how long should I wait before I start back breastfeeding? I've been pumping but I've been throwing it out."

"Hell I didn't breastfeed so I don't know. Maybe 24-48 hours I guess. I hope you got enough milk in the fridge while your ass getting drunk and shit. You ain't finna starve my grand baby."

"Whatever you say Ma. Well goodnight. Me and mama's baby are about to lay it down for the night. I'm damn tired."

"Umm I wonder what you did in Vegas…"

"DAD COME GET MAMA OUT OF MY ROOM!"

We both laugh before she kisses Mason on the forehead and leaves out of the room.

I lay him down in his basinet and then go in the bathroom to take a shower before bed. Today was truly exhausting and I was still tired as hell from this weekend's shenanigans.

After putting on my pajamas and tying up my hair, I turn my TV to Empire. Within five minutes I was dead to the world.

Slick

I knew it was gone be some shit once I got to work today and had to deal with this fuck ass nigga. His pussy ass kept walking by me mean mugging me like he wanted me to rock his shit again. I told myself that I was going to let it go until after work, but he just had to walk by me again.

"Ay homeboy is there a problem?" I question as I drop the tools I had in my hand.

"Yeah nigga the problem is you a snake. You played up under me the whole time just to make a move on my wife. You flaw as fuck dog. I will never fuck with you the same way again."

"Let's be clear you and I were never friends. We just fuckin work together."

"Ok glad you feel that way. Watch your back homeboy."

"Is that a threat cause we can settle whatever issue you got right here."

I step to him and everybody starts looking. I hear the supervisor telling us to break it up, but I wasn't hearing that shit. Mase had too much mouth and needed to be taught a fuckin lesson.

"Man come on. Whatever yall got going on needs to be handled outside of work. Don't let nobody fuck up your paper man," Jaylen tells me as he steps in between Mase and I.

I take his advice and walk back to my work station.

***

I was sitting outside at the lunch table with Rob and Jaylen. Mase was sitting at another table, but he just keeps watching me like I won't get up and rock his shit.

"So that's who the girl is that got you walking around open like a book. Damn Mase is pissed at you man," Rob says.

"So you went to Vegas with Shy and you couldn't even tell your best friend?" Jaylen questions.

"I just didn't have time for the negative comments."

"You know I'm always riding with you whether you right or wrong."

"Well do you think I'm wrong for falling in love with someone's who married."

"Biblically and morally yes, but we've all watched the way Mase treated her so it's no surprise that their marriage is over. If she makes you happy bruh then who am I to judge you."

"She's a great person. A way better upgrade from Chanel I tell you that much."

"I think anybody you date is an upgrade from Chanel," Rob jokes.

"She wasn't that bad now."

"AHHHH SHITTTT!"

We all laugh.

"Well since I got you two here. I need advice."

"Advice on what nigga."

"I want to make it official with Ashanti and pop the question."

"About fuckin time Jay. Eight years and three kids later and now you want to finally make it official. Hell, it was official after she popped out the first child."

"You know Slick has to be extra and give a whole speech."

"I'm just saying. It doesn't take a man forever to know if he wants to spend the rest of his life with a woman or not."

"But I wanted to wait until after she graduated college. Planning a wedding while studying for exams would've been nerve wrecking."

"Well I'm proud of you. So have you already gotten the ring?"

"No, but I got pictures of some choices. Tell me which ones yall think a woman would like."

He pulls out his phone and goes to the gallery. We look at three different choices for rings.

"I like the square shaped diamond," I announce.

"Yeah that was going to be my choice too."

"So when are you going to pop the question?"

"This weekend. I want us to go on a triple date. You know they have those romantic boat rides and you can book a slot. I booked it for three hours and I want you guys to come with us."

"Well you know Shy and I will be there."

"Desiree and I will be there too. Just be sure to give me a time and location so I can be sure to have a babysitter for that time."

"I got you. I should have everything finalized by Thursday."

"My boy stepping up and becoming a man. I'm proud of you Jay."

"Next step becoming a homeowner."

"Well if you need any help with that I got you a fire ass

realtor who helped me get my lot and a contracting company to build my house."

"My pockets aint as deep as yours you know I can't be going all out like you."

"As long as your credit score is in the 600s and you have had the same job for over a year then you should be good. Plus with your income and Ashanti's income, I'm pretty sure the banks will make some shake for you guys. They even have foreclosed homes that are remodeled going for the low. They are just trying to get rid of them as fast as possible so look into that."

"I appreciate that bro. You be looking out."

"What's the point in having knowledge if you're not going to share it with your brothers?"

***

After work, I go over to Shy parents' crib. They were all chilling in the den watching game shows. Mason was laying across Shy's lap on a blanket while she massages his scalp.

"Hey Mrs. Rissa and Mr. Derrick," I say as I take my seat on the couch next to shy.

"You make me sound so old just call me Rissa."

I lean over and give Shy a kiss.

"How was your day babe?"

"It was good. I took Mason for a walk in his stroller earlier. How was your day?"

"Other than the fact that Mase was at work on the same bullcrap, we got invited to go on a triple date this weekend. We will be having a romantic evening on a river boat."

"Sounds fun. With who though?"

"You remember Rob and Jaylen don't you."

"Yeah I might remember them. I don't know."

"Jaylen is going to propose to his girl, Ashanti. They've been together since they were 18."

"I'm stepping on that boat looking so sexy. You not gone be able to tell me nothing."

"We already can't tell you nothing," her mom responds.

"Oh quit being a hater all your life Ma."

"Do you fish Slick?"

"Yeah, but I haven't been in a while."

"Well I want you to come fishing with Shy's grandfather and I sometime. We usually go twice a month."

"Honey, they gone have you out there all day. Don't do it."

"You hush Rissa. You're just jealous cause your dad likes spending more time with me than you."

"Yeah cause I don't like fishing especially not with yall. We be out there from sun up to damn near dinner time. I don't have that type of time."

"But you will go to the spa and be there all day."

"Babe that's totally different."

Shy just looks at me and laughs.

"This is how they act all the time. You just gotta overlook them."

"Black love is a beautiful thing," I say.

"Only when it's done right."

"Come on babe let's go upstairs."

"Give me my grand baby before yall go."

"No, I'm putting him in his swinger. You are not about to have him spoiled rotten."

"Hell it's too late to say that. Give me my grand baby gul."

"Maaaa."

"I love you too now give him here."

She swaddles Mason in his blanket before passing him to her mother. I follow her upstairs to her room. She jumps in my arms as soon as the door closes.

"Babbbyyyy, I've missed you all day."

"I've missed you more."

We share a passionate kiss.

"Let's do a quickie."

"Hell na Shy your parents are downstairs."

"Babe come on."

"I don't even have a condom. We can go back to my place."

She jumps down out of my arms.

"You are staying with me tonight right?"

"Of course I am."

My cell phone vibrates and I pull it out of my pocket. It was a text from Mase.

And then your bitch ass be around my son. COUNT YOUR FUCKIN DAYS BITCH ASS NIGGA! AND TELL YOUR HOE I'M FIGHTING FOR FULL CUSTODY!

I clear out of the message and place my phone back in my pocket.

"Who was that? Don't tell me it was Chanel."

"Na. It was work related."

"Yeah I bet."

"Don't start that girl."

I pull her close and give her another kiss.

"You bringing Mason over the house tonight?"

"Na, I'll see if Ma will watch him. I'll just come home early in the morning when you leave for work."

"Yeah I'll let you keep the truck. You can just drop me off at work."

"Well let me grab some clothes. I'll meet your sexy ass downstairs."

I leave out of the room while she packs her an overnight bag.

On the way to my place, I stop by and grab some Chinese food.

"You wanna ride somewhere with me right quick?"

"Of course. I'll even ride you too."

"You're such a freak."

"But you like it though."

Twenty minutes later, I pull over to the side of the road and turn the car off.

"Where are we?"

"Get out the car and come on."

We both jump out of the car. I grab her hand and walk up on a lot where they were clearing off land to start construction.

"This is where our house is going to be."

"Our house?"

"You my girl right. What's mine is yours."

"This is a nice piece of land."

I pull out my phone and show her pictures of the house.

"Babe this is beautiful. You got some good taste. I'm happy for you."

"No, I'm happy for us."

"How many bedrooms?"

"5 bedrooms, but I want to turn the basement into a bedroom."

"Why not make it a man cave? You deserve something for yourself since the rest of the house is going to be mine."

"Oh is that so?"

I pick her up and we kiss.

"I love you woman."

"I love you too man."

Shy

For the past couple of days, someone has been playing on my phone. I didn't tell Slick cause I already knew he would nut up about it. I already knew it was Mase's stupid ass. He was still in his feelings about me talking to Slick. His ass should've did right by me and we wouldn't be in this predicament to begin with.

Right now I am getting dressed to go out on a couple's date with Slick and his boys. I had on a burgundy body con dress with gold heels and gold earrings. Slick was sitting on the bed just watching me in the mirror.

"How many times are you going to change your outfit? You look fine."

"I'm sticking with this one babe I promise."

"Thank you. I was ready an hour ago."

"I'm sorry babe. I just want to make a great first impression."

"The only person whose opinion matters is mine and I love you even when your hair is tied and you're chilling with my baggy t shirt on."

"That's why I love your chocolate ass," I inform him.

"Well love me enough to grab your purse so we can leave before the boat leaves us."

"Yes sir Daddy Slick."

"You gone be saying that all night just keep on."

I take one last look at myself before grabbing my gold clutch and my phone. I follow Slick outside to his truck. Lo and behold, this bitch Chanel was sitting on the hood. I don't know who was more crazy, her or Mase.

"Damn so you just gone leave your girl and child for another bitch?"

"Chanel, you got two seconds to get the fuck off my truck or I'm snatching your ass off."

"Really Slick this is how you do me and your child?"

"My child is dead remember. You had an abortion behind my back. Will you please quit harassing me and just move the fuck on? Where is Nathan? Damn did he get tired of your ass too?"

"Slick please let me beat this bitch ass just one time."

"Who ass you gone beat?" she questions as she jumps down for the hood.

"Baby hold my stuff."

"Shy you are not about to fight. Chanel leave before I call the police."

"You are foul Slick. I guarantee you that she will never

fuck you and suck you like I did. You are going to miss this pussy and I'm not taking you back either."

"Ok that's fine Chanel. Can you just go?"

She lunges at me and Slick pulls me behind him.

"Oh so you her bodyguard now?"

"Bitch, I will fuck you up. You lucky Slick keeps sparing your ugly ass. You got one more time to pop up and then I'm beating your ass. And I put that on my mama."

Slick unlocks his truck and walks me over to the passenger's side. He opens the door so that I could get in. The whole time Chanel was still standing there running off at the mouth. I was ready to bop her ass one good time, but I was looking too damn sexy in this dress to be fighting her crazy ass. While Slick was walking around to get in the driver's seat, her ass fell to the ground on her knees.

"SLICK PLEASE I'M SORRY BABE. I PROMISE I'LL DO RIGHT THIS TIME. IT'S HURTING MY HEART TO SEE YOU WITH SOMEONE ELSE. I LOVE YOU."

He looks at her, gets in the car, and starts the engine. While backing out of the parking space, she picks up some rocks and throws them at his truck.

"That bitch is fuckin delusional. If the dick gone have me acting like that, I don't want it anymore."

He looks at me and laughs.

"Babe, you're laughing and I'm dead ass serious. That bitch is crazy. What the fuck was you doing to her? Jesus."

"I don't want her to ruin our night. That was probably her goal anyway."

"It's gone take more than a crazy ex-girlfriend to make me leave you alone. You are all mine now. She should've played her cards right."

***

We link up with everyone at the loading dock. After introducing ourselves to one another, we head onto the boat. We take our seats at a table before the hostess brings us some drinks.

"I heard you just had a baby Shy," Ashanti says.

"Yeah he's eight weeks now."

"After having three kids, I do not miss waking up in the middle of the night to fix bottles."

"Well in my case I'm breastfeeding so I just have to pop this boob out and let him have his way."

"Is it way better than using the canned milk?"

"Hell yeah. It's more healthier. It gives them all of the nutrients that they need while they are young. My baby was premature weighing only 5 pounds and 2 oz. Now he's a little over 8 pounds which the doctors say is great. He's gaining weight faster than they expected."

"That's a blessing. My twin boys are 6 and my daughter is 3."

"Do you have any kids Desiree?"

"Yes two and that's a fuckin nough."

"Don't say it like that now. My babies aint bad."

"I didn't say they were bad, but shit is stressful when you barely have fuckin help. I'm done. I do not want any more."

"How old are they?"

"Girl they 4 and 5 years old. I had my kids back to back like an ass."

"Well I hope you want more kids Shy cause I do."

"Who said I was having more kids Slick?"

"Me."

"So Slick tells me you and Jaylen been together eight years."

"Girl yes. Eight years and three kids later and I still don't have a ring. Isn't that something?"

"Don't you start now Ashanti."

"Well I'm just saying. I'm not trying to be 50 years old before you finally decide you wish to get married."

"You will not be 50 I promise."

"40 neither hell."

"Yall are so cute together. I love it."

"Girl he works my nerves, but he's a great man and a great father."

"Everybody all in love tonight. How cute?"

"You're so lame Rob."

"I'm glad to see my boy with someone who makes him happy. He needed something real after the past relationships he's had."

"So relationship question how often should couples have sex?" Jaylen asks.

"Every day," Slick and I answer simultaneously.

"Who the hell has the energy to have sex every day? I'm a nurse so I don't have that type of time nor energy. I say three times a week or maybe two at the least," Ashanti answers.

"Shit I'm with you. I don't have the energy nor the desire to be hunching every day. You'd be lucky to get it once a week."

"That once a week aint cutting it Desiree. A man has needs."

"Well I need for you to help out with the kids more and then I can cater to your needs. Relationships are a two way street. Don't start that."

"She does have a point. As a former house wife, it was tiring just going to school, cleaning up, and then having a big dinner prepared every night. Men have to meet us halfway sometimes. Shit, we get tired too."

"You were married before? Girl you look like a baby."

"I'm 21," I answer.

"Still a baby."

"She's my baby though."

Slick pulls me close and kisses me on the forehead.

After a few appetizers and drinks, we have a slow dance. Luther Vandross *Can I Take You Out Tonight?* was playing.

"What you know about Luther girl?"

"Don't act like I'm just super young now Slick."

"I love you baby."

"Do you really or are you just saying that?"

"I wouldn't lie to you. I really love you Shy. It's just something about you that speaks to my spirit. I wish that I had met you sooner so that I could love you longer."

"Don't you make me start crying now."

"Yes ma'am."

He pulls me into a kiss and I wrap my arms around his neck.

Eric Benet's *Spend My Life With You* starts playing which apparently was their cue that Jaylen was getting ready to propose. Rob and Slick stop dancing while Jaylen and Ashanti have the floor.

It was so cute watching him sing to her while they danced.

"Baby do you love me?" he questions her.

"Of course, I do."

He gets down on one knee and pulls out the ring box. She was hysterical before he even opens the box.

"Jaylen.."

"I love you Ashanti. I've been wanting to do this for

quite some time now. I'm not afraid to admit that I was scared. I just don't want marriage to change our relationship. Life wouldn't be the same if we weren't together. I just want to spend the rest of my life with you. Would you do me the honor of being my wife?"

"Hell yes baby."

He barely had time to put the ring on her finger before she pulls him up into a kiss. We all stand around and clap. It was so beautiful seeing two people in love. I look at Slick who was smiling from ear to ear.

Slick

While Shy was still sleeping, I was in the kitchen cooking her a nice breakfast while listening to Sir Charles Jones radio on Pandora.

"Baby if you want my loving, tell me how you want it tonight."

I was standing in front of the stove flipping an omelet when I hear giggling. I turn to see Shy standing there in nothing but a tank top and some panties.

I walk over to her still singing. I pull her close to me and we dance around the kitchen.

"You must be in a good mood babe."

"Yes because I woke up next to the most beautiful woman in the world."

"Let me be the smile on your face and I'll be your stars and your moon. I wanna be your sunny day. Can I be your favorite tune? I wanna be your breakfast in bed and I'll be your fool. Mr. Too Damn Good To You."

I spin her around just as I had to go take the food off the stove. She comes up behind me and wraps her arms around me. She kisses all over my back.

"Don't start nothing that you can't finish," I tell her.

"You know me better than that Slick."

"So what are you going to do?"

There was a knock on my front door.

"I hope this ain't Chanel's ass again Slick because if it is she getting beat the fuck up today."

He walks to the peephole and looks out.

"It's my mother."

"Well I'll be in the back room babe."

"Ok."

I watch Shy walk off to the bedroom. I wait until the door is closed before I let my mom in.

"Damn you don't believe in putting on clothes do you?"

"Considering the fact that I'm in my own apartment the answer is no. Good morning to you too."

"Something smells good."

She takes a seat at the bar while I walk back in the kitchen.

"You must have company?"

"Ma, what brings you over here this early in the morning."

"Damn, I can't come check on my son. I haven't heard from ya. I figured you must've gotten back with that ol Chanel."

"Na Chanel and I are not back together?"

"So who's the other plate for?"

"Well my girlfriend and I were preparing to have a romantic breakfast."

"Why haven't I met her yet?"

"Because you're so judgmental."

"Na I just tell you the truth and you hate hearing it."

"Ok so what's up Ma?"

"I need some money."

"I'm broke."

"You were just in Vegas last weekend."

"Please don't count my pockets."

"You taking females on trips, but can't loan your own mother some money."

"A loan would mean I'll get it back, but I never do. I just paid your mortgage and your utilities. Where is all your money going? Why you can't ask that dude that be sneaking over there all the time? You preaching to me about the type of women I attract, but you're doing the same with these men. Every other week, it's a new bill. You get unemployment and child support. Where is that going?"

"So you're really not going to help your mother out after all I have done for you Solomon?"

I suck my teeth.

"Wait right here."

I go in the bedroom and close the door. Shy was on the bed watching cartoons. I go to the closet and pull out a shoebox. I grab three crisp hundred dollar bills and walk back in the kitchen.

"Make this your last time."

"Oh whatever. My own damn son got a problem with helping out his mama."

"I don't have a problem with helping you, but why is that nigga not helping you. You are too grown to be letting a man play in you and not pay you."

She gets off the barstool and leaves out of my apartment.

My mom had a history of taking care of bum ass niggas and she wonders where I get it from.

***

After having our breakfast date in the den, Shy and I get in the shower together so we could head to the mall. She gets on her knees and slides my dick in her warm mouth.

"I guess I gotta cook you breakfast more often if I can get head like this."

She plays with my head with her tongue as she strokes my shaft with her left hand.

"I swear you be tryna turn a nigga out."

She was sucking the life out of me right now. I was trying not to bust in her mouth, but she was singing on my dick as if it was a microphone.

"Shyyyyyyyy……"

She pulls my dick out of her mouth just as it erupts with cum.

She was bent over in the full body mirror touching her toes while I was beating her pussy up from behind. I grab ahold of her ponytail while I'm stroking the fuck out of her pussy. The more she moans my name, the more turned on I was becoming.

"Don't stop babe."

"Trust me I'm not," I say while smacking her ass.

"FUCK ME BABY! MY GOD!"

"Tell me it's good girl."

"YESSS BAE IT'S GOOD!"

"You like it?"

"I LOVE IT. SHIITTTTT!"

I knew her ass was going to do that. She explodes which causes me to do the same. I pull off the condom and go in the bathroom to flush it.

"Damn, you be putting it down."

She walks back in the bathroom and turns on the shower water.

"I'm ready to go home and see my baby now."

"See how you do.. Just get my good dick and leave."

She laughs before stepping into the shower and I follow suit.

Shy

"Hey mama's baby," I say kissing Mason under his chin and on his neck.

"You missed me cause I sho been missing you."

He was just smiling and showing off his big hazel eyes.

"Mommy loves you Mason."

My cell phone rings and I see it was his dad calling.

"Hello."

"Ay I'm coming to get Mason for a few hours."

"Umm it's a thing called asking. You just don't tell me you're coming to get my child."

"Hoe that's my child too."

"See you damn sho aint getting him now. Fuck you."

"Be expecting a paper from the courts Shy. I'm getting full custody of my child. Your ass aint never with him anyway. Too busy out sucking and fucking on the next nigga. Couldn't even give me my last name back first."

"FUCK YOU MASE!"

"NA HOE IT'S FUCK YOU. YOU GONE REGRET WHAT THE FUCK YOU DID. I BET YOU THAT SHY."

"GO SUCK A DICK MASE!"

I press the end button and block his number. That bastard had some nerve talking about fighting for custody when he was the one cheated and neglected me while I was pregnant.

"Excuse me for cursing Mason, but your daddy is an asshole."

He was just so tickled at me saying that. I lean down and kiss him on the nose.

"You are smart. You are kind. You are important. You are blessed. Remember that ok and don't let nobody tell you otherwise. Always know that your mama loves you no matter what anyone else says."

I kiss him on the nose one more time.

***

The next afternoon my parents and I were out sitting on the porch playing Dominoes while Mason was in his swinger sucking his pacifier like it was nobody's business.

Out of nowhere two police cars and a silver Impala pull up. The police jump out like they were here to arrest somebody. My father stands up and walks to the edge of the porch.

"May I help you officers?"

Two females walks up to my father.

"We're with the Department of Human Resources. We received a call this morning regarding child neglect and child endangerment."

"From who?"

"We can't reveal that information, but we are here to take a look at the child and to do a walk-through of the home."

"You gotta be fuckin kidding me?"

"I'm afraid not sir."

"Jefferson you know me and you know my family. What type of crap is this?" my father says to one of the officers.

"I understand your frustrations, but we're just here to do our job. It's nothing personal. We have to follow up regarding every call we receive whether we want too or not."

"Can I take a look around the house specifically his sleeping area and play area?"

"Shy go in the house and show her around while your father and I talk with these people."

I was trying to reach for Mason but one of the women stopped me.

"You can leave him. I will need to take a look to check for any signs of abuse or neglect."

I give her a nasty glare before following the woman inside of the house. I take her upstairs to my bedroom and my adjacent bathroom. She flips the light switch to make sure the lights were on and then turns on the water faucet.

"I know you're frustrated ma'am, but I'm just doing my job. If we get a call, we have to take it serious until we conclude our investigation."

"It's nobody's doing but my low down husband. Well soon to be nothing once this marriage is annulled. He's a complete jack ass just trying to make my life a living hell."

"Trust me we get calls like these all the time where one parent calls DHR on the other just to avoid paying child support or just out of spite. I'm sorry that this happened to you."

"Yeah I'm sorry too. Sorry that I wasted six years of my life with a low down bastard."

"Can you show me the kitchen area where you keep his bottles and formula?"

I lead her back downstairs and into the kitchen.

"This is a nice kitchen. I love the marble countertops."

"I breastfeed so he doesn't have formula but his bottles are kept in this cabinet and in the refrigerator."

She takes a few notes on her notepad.

"Well this concludes my search. Let's go back outside."

I follow her back out onto the porch.

"Everything inside looks good. I see no signs that he's being neglected or mistreated."

"Sorry to bother you. I got your number so I will be doing a home check again soon just to get an update."

They all leave.

"When I see that muthafucka I'm beating his ass. He really has gone too far this time. Once you bring the police to my front door step, it's a fuckin problem. And you got these folks thinking Mason is being neglected. He deserves a well whooped ass," my father fusses as he storms in the house.

"My goodness I need a drink," my mom says as she follows him.

***

Slick, Mason, and I were out to eat at Shrimp Basket for dinner. I had been super emotional all day and I didn't want to sit in that house any longer.

"So are you gone finally tell me what's been bothering you? I can tell you've been crying."

"Mase called DHR on me and had them come out to my parent's house."

"SHY CAN I JUST BEAT HIS ASS ONE MORE TIME PLEASE?"

"Bae."

"I'M TIRED OF HIM FUCKING WITH YOU."

"Calm down babe. I don't have too much longer to deal with his ass."

"I'm checking him tomorrow at work and I'm not playing."

"I wanted to go out so I wouldn't have to think about all that drama right now."

"I'm sorry. You want to go out of town this weekend just the two of us? We can leave Friday for the beach."

"You are supposed to be saving money right now Slick."

"Don't worry about me I got this and I got us."

"Ok then big baller."

"So have you thought about going back to school yet?"

"Yeah. I want to go back in the fall but I don't know what major I want to study. I wanted to be a teacher but they don't pay enough."

"Well what is that you like to do? Nurses pay good. I think Ashanti has her Bachelors of Science in Nursing if I'm not mistaken."

"I've never thought about that. I don't know if I like people well enough to want to be a nurse."

"Well just look online at different degrees and see what it is that you may be interested in. As long as it doesn't have you working late hours. I need you home with me at night so I can rub on your booty."

I look at him and laugh.

"You're crazy. So have they given you a deadline for the house?"

"Yes they told me 3-6 months. I'm hoping between 3 and 4 months so we could be moved in by the holidays."

"Yeah our first Christmas together will be awesome."

"Yeah because I'm spoiling the hell out of you for Christmas."

"I wonder what I'm getting."

"It might be a gift. It might be a trip. You just never

know."

"You're so unpredictable."

"But you love it though."

"Hell yeah I do."

Mason starts whining for something to eat so I pop out my boob and start to breastfeed, but not before covering us up with a blanket.

"I love seeing you in mommy mode. It's so sexy to me."

"Really Slick?"

"Yes. I've always wanted kids. It still hurts knowing I could've been a father this year."

"Just thank God he spared you from a crazy ass baby mama."

"Are you going to be the mother of my children one day?"

"It's possible, but I don't want to rush anything right now. Let us take our time."

"Ok. I can see you wobbling around our big house pregnant and fussing."

"Why I gotta be fussing? I'm an angel."

"Yeah until you get mad."

Even with everything that was going on in my life, Slick could find a way to make everything so much better. I just stare at him with a big smile plastered on my face while he eats his food.

He was everything I ever dreamed of having in a man. He was a gentlemen, but he still had a little street in him. He could sing. He could dance. He didn't mind showing me off in public and telling me how beautiful I was. And when he spoke on the future, he always included my son and I in his plans. Every moment that we were together still feels like the very first time we kicked it. I was just head over heels in love with this man.

"What you over there thinking about? You smiling pretty hard."

"Just thinking on how much I appreciate you for coming into my life and showing me that all men are not the same."

"I have a lot more in store for you babe. As long as you're loyal and honest with me, I will give you the world no questions asked."

***

After dinner, we went back to his apartment. I give Mason a nice warm bath in his lavender sleep body wash before breastfeeding him and rocking him to sleep. We give Msaon the bed and we make us a pallet on the floor in the den.

He was massaging my feet while we watch *Night School* with Kevin Hart and Tiffany Haddish. He brings my foot up to his mouth and he kisses it.

"When you first saw me what was the first thought that came to mind?"

"Damn he's so chocolate and handsome with perfect white teeth."

"The first time I ever really payed attention to you was when I saw you dancing in the kitchen while pregnant. Your spirit just pulls me in and wants me to get more and more of you."

"Have you ever thought about getting married?"

"Yes. I always wanted to get married, but I just never found the woman that screamed *MARRY ME* up until now. You have wife written all over you. The last man that had you just couldn't read."

I pull him in for a kiss. One peck led to another. Next thing I know he was sliding off my panties wanting to get a mouth full of my candy.

I open my legs wide as he gets down in between my legs. He teases me at first by planting kisses all over my juicy lips. He sucks on them a few times and then spreads them apart.

I place my hand on his head so he could not move as I

lift up my hips. I was getting hornier with every suck and lick.

"Yesss babyyy."

He pushes my legs up to my head while sliding his tongue in and out of my pussy. I feel his tongue slide down to my ass.

"Oh my Godddddddddddddd. Oh baby that feels so fuckin good."

I was in heaven right now. Tears begin to slide down my face as he gives me a whole new high.

Now I see why his ex bitch was going crazy over him.

Shy

The next morning when I wake up Slick had already left for work. Mason was now in the den with me sitting in his rocker watching Winnie the Pooh on the cartoon channel.

I get up and go to the fridge to grab a bottle of water. I see a note on the bar.

Good morning beautiful.
I left you my truck for today. I caught Jaylen to work. Here's my card. Go spoil yourself. When I said I'd give you the world, I meant it. You deserve it. Check your texts for the pin number to my card. I fed Mason one of the bottles you had pumped last night.

P.S. Ashanti wants to hang out today. Text her 713-346-5671
I love you.

I go in the bathroom and draw me a bath using a Eucalyptus scented bath bomb. I grab my phone and shoot Slick a text.

Good morning sexy. Thank you. I can't wait to see you when you get off.

I turn on my slow jam mix and place my phone on the counter before getting in the bath tub.

***

Ashanti and I were out at the mall doing a little shopping. She was pushing her daughter Sanai in her stroller while I had Mason in his stroller as well.

"So how does it feel to be engaged girl?"

"Girl I couldn't be happier. I've always wanted to spend the rest of my life with Jaylen. He has his faults, but I can't deny that he is a provider, a great father, and a great friend. He makes sure our household is straight before anything."

"And that's all that matters. I'm happy for you."

"If you don't mind me asking why did you separate from your husband?"

"After six years of getting cheated on, neglected, and mistreated you'd leave too."

"Yeah you got that right. You deserve way more. You're too beautiful and too young to be settling for that. Don't let people make you feel for walking away from an unhealthy situation."

"Girl trust me fuck these folks opinions. I'm living my best life and I'm truly happy. I'm back close to my family, my child is healthy, and I got a man who adores the hell out of me. What more can a girl ask for?"

"You got that right. After six years of getting cheated on,

I would've been left too hell. Niggas be wanting you to hold them down while they only giving mediocre dick, lies, and headaches. Women are not putting up with that shit no more."

"You got that right cause I'd be a fool to constantly take you back if I gotta pull up on you at another bitch house just to make you come home."

"Oh hell na now he wrong for that. Wish I would've known you then. Girl we would've been pulling up together. I would've pepper sprayed his ass."

"I'm so over him," I say looking at some boots in Nordstrom.

"What month would be a good month to have a wedding?"

"Between April and August if you ask me. That way you can have an outside wedding or at least an outside cocktail hour and reception."

"True."

"Our parents are super excited about helping us plan."

"Do yall parents like each other?"

"Girl they love each other. Our mothers talk on the phone damn near every day."

"That's a blessing."

I pay for the boots and then we head into another store.

"Let's go into that sex store. Slick and I are going on a weekend getaway Friday."

"Girl yall stay going somewhere. Shit, I need your life."

"Girl you don't want it. Trust me. It's stressful as hell."

We head into the sex store and I see so many fun things I wanted to get for Slick. I was like a kid in a candy store. I was picking up any and everything.

"The vibrating dick ring is the truth. Yall will love that. Get some handcuffs. You can never go wrong with those."

"You and Jaylen need to take some time off so yall can go off somewhere just the two of you. Trust me every couple needs alone time. Never feel bad for leaving your kids so you can enjoy yourself and have a little peace of mind."

"You right. I think Imma plan something for us cause if I leave it up to him, it would never get done. He is not good at making plans or reservations."

I grab a couple of things to spice up our upcoming weekend before we go into Body Central and then Fashion Metro.

After spending a day of shopping and having lunch inside of the food court together, we go our separate ways.

I get outside to the truck only to find that someone had purposely slit his tire.

"FUCKKKKK!!"

Damn, I just couldn't catch a break.

***

After Slick had someone to come and replace the tire, I go back to his apartment and cook him dinner. I had some shit up my sleeve tonight so I was going to feed him good, fuck him good, and then put his ass to sleep.

He arrives home from work. I had him a nice bubble bath ran. We eat, watch a movie together, and then fuck. Once Mason and him were both knocked out cold, I crept off to pay Mase a visit. I was getting sick and tired of him fucking with me so tonight was payback.

I arrive at the house I once shared with my husband to see an additional car in the driveway. His nasty ass must got company. I look under the flower pot for the spare key before letting myself inside the back door. I disarm the alarm system before it goes off.

It was pitch black. I creep through the kitchen and up the stairs. Once I get to the bedroom door, I hear moaning and the sounds of someone having sex.

I bust in and turn the lights on. Mase jumps up ready to swing at whoever was at the door. I look past him and see my cousin Terrica lying in bed trying to cover herself up.

"REALLY TERRICA? REALLY?"

"Shy, I can explain."

"WHY THE FUCK YOU IN MY HOUSE ANYWAY?"

Before I could think, I swing my bat at his ass.

"ARE YOU FUCKIN CRAZY?"

"YES. YES THE FUCK I AM. YOU AND YOUR
BITCH FINNA FIND OUT JUST HOW CRAZY I AM!"

Mase jumps back as I keep swinging at his ass with my
iron bat.

"SHY GET THE FUCK OUT BEFORE I CALL THE
POLICE."

"OH LIKE YOU DID WHEN YOU CALLED DHR
AND TOLD THEM I WAS PUTTING OUR CHILD IN
DANGER. YOU ARE A LOW DOWN PIECE OF SHIT
MASE."

"I DIDN'T CALL DHR ON YOU."

"YOU A MUTHAFUCKIN LIE. WHO THE FUCK
ELSE DID IT? YOU ARE A LOW DOWN DIRTY ASS
NIGGA AND THEN YOU LAYING UP WITH MY
DAMN COUSIN."

"SO. DON'T YOU GOTTA MAN?"

"YOU GOT TWO SECONDS TO MAKE THIS BITCH LEAVE OR I'M BEATING YOUR ASS MASE."

"HOW YOU GONE PUT SOMEBODY OUT MY DAMN HOUSE? YOU DONE LOST YOUR FUCKIN MIND."

I swing and bust the lamp by his bed.

"YOUR TV IS NEXT."

Out of the corner of my eye, I see Terrica trying to run out of the room with her clothes in hand. I grab her by her weave and slam her into the wall. She screams and grabs her nose.

"BITCH YOU LOW DOWN AS FUCK. YOU A LOW DOWN ASS HOE."

I push her ass out of the room before slamming the door in her face.

"YOU REALLY GOT SOME NERVE MASE."

"YOU LAID UP WITH MY HOMEBOY, BUT I'M THE ONE TRIPPING."

"AFTER ALL YOU'VE PUT ME THROUGH, YOU WENT AND FUCKED MY OWN FLESH AND BLOOD. YOU'RE A SNAKE MASE."

I lose my mind and I go on a rampage. I tore the master bedroom up with my bat. When he tried to take it from me, I swung and hit him in the knee caps. He fell down in pain.

"YOU CRAZY BITCH."

"OH YOU HAVE NOT SEEN CRAZY YET. EVERY CHANCE I GET, I'M MAKING YOUR LIFE HELL. I'M COMING TO YOUR JOB. I'M POPPING UP ON YOU AT THE GAS STATION. EVERY TIME I SEE YOU WITH A BITCH, I'M SHOWING MY ASS. I ASKED YOU TO LEAVE ME THE FUCK ALONE, BUT YOU JUST COULDN'T. WHY? WHAT HAVE I DONE TO YOU? HUH MASE? I GAVE YOU MY FUCKIN VIRGINITY AND THIS IS THE TYPE OF SHIT I HAVE TO DEAL WITH FROM YOU."

He tries to get up and grab the bat from me, but I back away. I open the room door and run down the stairs and out the front door. I didn't stop running until I was at Slick's truck. I jump in and pull off down the street just as I watch Mase hopping out the front door.

I just couldn't believe my own cousin would go behind my back and fuck my husband. He was flaw and her nasty ass was too.

But payback was coming. Two could play this game, but I was gone play this shit a helluva lot better.

Slick

It was Wednesday afternoon and I was just getting off work. On my way home, Shy's dad calls me out the blue and asks can we link up for beer and wings at the bar by their house in an hour. Of course I said yeah, but I was wondering what the hell this was all about.

I arrive home to my empty apartment since Shy had stayed at her parents last night. I shower, change clothes, and head across town to meet up with Derrick.

"So how are things with you and my daughter?"

"They are great. I couldn't wish for better."

The server comes and brings us two beers and an appetizer of buffalo chicken dip before walking to the next table to get their requests.

"I can tell you're going to be around for a long time. I really like the fact that you've been making my daughter happy."

"Your daughter is a good woman and she deserves to be treated as such."

"Yeah that's my princess. If you hurt her, you know I'm going to kill you right?"

"Well I will keep that in mind sir."

"The real reason I asked you out for drinks is because I have a business proposition for you."

"Ok and what is that?"

"I want you to run drugs for me."

I choke on my beer.

"What?"

"You heard me correctly. I know you're already in the drug game. I've done my homework on you. Since you like to travel, you can help me move weight from here to Florida and from here to Cali."

"What's in it for me?"

"I assure you that you will be well compensated."

"Does Shy know any of this?"

"That her parents are kingpins. Hell no. And don't let her find out."

"Well since we're here, what are we going to do about Mase? I've been trying to spare him since he's your grandson's father, but he taking this shit too far."

"I got something planned for him. Just be patient. You and Shy are going to Miami this weekend right?"

"Yea that's the plan."

"Ok all you have to do when you get to Florida is make sure the package makes it from one location to the other. The money will be wired once you make it happen."

"Ok that's a bet."

"I got connections in Florida just in case something goes wrong. Don't be afraid to call me."

Before we could finish our beers, his cell phone rings. He answers it and could hear screaming from the other end of the phone.

"Calm down. I'm on the way."

He ends the call.

"Come on. We gotta go. Follow me back to the house."

He throws some money on the table and we dip out.

I pull up on the curb to their house and see Shy, her mom, and two people that I recognized from her baby shower.

"BITCH YOU LOW DOWN AS FUCK."

I go swoop up Shy and carry her back in the house.

"What's wrong with you?"

I put her down and she just stands there ready to cry.

"I'm your man talk to me. What happened?"

"She's fuckin Mase. She's supposed to be my damn cousin Slick. He just keeps finding a way to hurt me."

She just stands there and cry in her hands.

"Shy, do you want to be with me?"

"Of course I do. What type of question is that?"

"Well quit letting Mase get under your skin. That's what he wants to do. If she wants to lay up with his trifling ass, let her have him. She aint got herself shit. You know it. I know it. And he knows it too. You have a child now. You can't be out here fighting and going off the deep end when he's already called DHR and got an open case on you. Think smarter babe."

"But Slick."

"Na aint no buts. I'm not gone tell you nothing wrong. If you want me to beat his ass, just say the word and I will."

"Babe can I just beat her ass one good time. I owe it to myself."

"Hell no. Now go grab Mason and meet me in the truck. You're staying with me tonight."

"I like it when you say it like that."

"Yeah I bet you do."

I kiss her on the forehead before she goes upstairs and I go back outside.

"Your daughter needs to control her damn temper Rissa. Look at Terrica's nose."

"Well I'm not saying she deserved it, but just know I understand where my child is coming from."

"Yeah of course you'd understand, you are where she gets it from."

"Just like you're riding for your daughter, I will always ride for mine. I'm not going to tell her how to feel when your daughter is sleeping with a man she spent all of her teenage years with. Out of all the men in Texas, you had to sleep with Mase and after all of the pain he has put this family through."

"Your daughter is married with a boyfriend, but we not gone address that now are we."

"Lorraine, you got more time to throw a slick shot at my child and it's gone be me and you with the problem."

"Yeah whatever I'm calling Dad to let him know how ignorant his grandchild is out here acting."

"Make sure you let him know that your daughter is a hoe

like you were back in the day. Let's not forget that I raised your child while you were out running the streets."

"Screw you LaRissa and your criminal ass husband."

"At least I have a husband and what do you have?"

"A degree. Don't come for me LaRissa cause I will read you for filth. You swear you so above everybody because you live in the nice house and because you don't work. You still aint shit."

"Well thank you Lorraine. I'm glad to know how you really feel. Maybe I would've had time to get a degree if you didn't throw your child off on me and take off for months at a time. The least you could've did was come back with a degree cause you damn sho didn't come back with no money."

"Everybody can't be selling drugs like you and your husband."

"WELL ATLEAST I AINT SELLING PUSSY! DO YOU WANT ME TO GIVE YOU A JOB?"

"FUCK YOU LARISSA. FUCK YOU."

"GET THE FUCK OFF MY PROPERTY! GET THE FUCK OFF MY PROPERTY BITCH!"

She and her daughter gets in the car and leave.

Rissa goes in the house and slams the door.

"I guess that's my cue to go and grab another beer," Derrick says to no one in particular.

What type of dysfunctional family did I get myself into?

Shy

After today's events, I just wanted to soak in this nice warm bubble bath and relax. Despite what Slick says, I was still gone beat that bitch to sleep. I was tired of sparing these hoes. She was gone have to give me my one. Either she was gone beat my ass or I was gone beat hers, but she was gone have to see me.

I look up and see Slick standing in the bathroom door drinking a beer.

"Care to join me?"

"You don't have to ask me twice."

He strips naked and sits behind me in the tub. He kisses me on my neck.

"I love you Slick."

"You better cause I love you too."

"We should go triple dating again. I want to go horseback riding this time."

"Horseback riding."

"Yes, it'll be fun babe. I always wanted to do that. We need to go to the aquarium together one day too and the zoo."

"Ok I can make it happen."

"I need me a job cause I be wanna do too much."

"Just take you a break until school starts back in August."

"I think I should cause I've never worked a day in my life. I wouldn't know where to start."

"Really?"

"Yeah. I think I should get a job though. I can get to meet new people cause I have no friends whatsoever. I don't even have any social media pages."

"Well I can't talk I don't have any either. I had a Facebook, but I forgot the damn password."

"Good cause I don't need no hoes inboxing you trying to shoot their shot."

"I don't want no one but you. A thousand girls could try to talk to me and I'd still say the same thing. I'm not letting you go Shy."

I turn around and straddle his lap.

"Thank you for being such a good man to me. I know I come with a lot of baggage, but I appreciate you for sticking around."

"Nobody's perfect, but you're perfect for me."

I kiss him and before I could pull away, he slips in some tongue.

***

It was Friday morning and I was on my way to the airport with Slick. Mase's mom had called earlier in the week begging to keep Mason so I used this opportunity to drop him off with her for the weekend.

Slick and I stop by Chick-fil-A to grab breakfast before hitting the interstate. Calvin Richardson starts playing on the radio and Slick begins to sing.

"In one million years, I never thought I'd meet someone that's perfect. I never thought that someone could make my mind go round in circles. I never thought there was a beach with jet black sand in Jersey. Like my legs, I can't walk around without you. Like my heart, the rhythm's bound to change without you. The way it beats, tapping on my mind. When I think about you girl holding on, I can't let go of you."

He grabs my hand and kisses it.

Out of nowhere, I hear a loud boom as a car runs us off the highway. Slick tries to keep control of the wheel, but the truck flips and flips.

The last thing I remember is hearing Slick's voice telling me he was going to get me out.

I was in and out of consciousness.

When I come to, I was looking up at a bunch of people staring down at me while they were pushing me on a stretcher.

"Is she going to be ok?" I hear my mom ask.

"HER BLOOD PRESSURES DROPPING. GET HER INTO THE O.R. NOW."

I fall back asleep hearing Slick's voice replaying in my head.

"When I think about you girl holding on, I can't let go of you."

Slick

I had a few scratches and a few bruises, but for the most part I was ok. I was only worried about Shy and if she was going to be alright.

On our way to the airport, a car ran a red light and hit us from the side causing the car to flip repeatedly before landing in a ditch. It was a miracle that I was able to get out and walk. Shy on the other hand was stuck in the car and emergency personnel had to cut her out.

She was now in emergency surgery and I was going crazy just pacing back and forth in the waiting room.

"You should go and get checked out Slick," her mom tells me.

"I'm ok. I'll be fine."

A nurse walks in the waiting room carrying a clipboard.

"Have you heard anything nurse?"

"Not at the moment. She's still in the OR. As soon as we know something, I will relay that information to you guys."

"I do have a few questions. I don't mean to come off as being insensitive, but these are questions that we have to ask. In the event that something happens, who is the next of kin?"

"I'm her husband," Mase answers.

'Not for long," Rissa answers.

"Well as of right now, I'm still her husband."

"You will not be making any decisions regarding my child. You are low down and conniving."

"Rissa, now is not the time nor the place. We're in a hospital and Shy is in surgery," Derricks informs her

"He's not about to pull the plug on my child to try and collect a check."

"Don't get it twisted, I don't need no insurance money. I wouldn't want to kill the mother of my damn child."

"Don't play that innocent roll. You just called DHR on her trying to get them to take Mason away."

I get up and walk out of the waiting room. This was just too much for me. I didn't want to be spending my day at the hospital not knowing if my girl was going to live or die. We were supposed to be on the beach right now.

It's funny how life never goes as planned.

"I'm sick of him Derrick," I hear Larissa saying as they were walking outside.

"We have got to keep it together for Shy's sake."

He pulls her into a hug and she breaks down crying on his chest.

"She's our only child," she says in between sobs.

Hearing her cry breaks my heart.

I really didn't want to be at this hospital any longer. I catch a cab home so I could shower and get out of these dirty, bloody clothes.

***

I was back at the hospital. Shy had come out of surgery but she was heavily sedated and hooked up to a lot of different machines.

I go in her room and take a seat beside the bed. I grab her hand and kiss it.

"I've looked for love in all the same old places. Found the bottom of a bottle always dry. But when you poured out your heart I didn't waste it cause there's nothing like your love to get me high. You're as smooth as Tennessee whiskey. You're as sweet as strawberry wine. You're as warm as a glass of brandy. And honey, I stay stoned on your love all the time."

I look up to see Mase standing in the doorway.

"Why are you here?"

"She's my wife in case you forgot."

"How could we forget Mase? You treated her life shit. She wouldn't even want you here."

"You're real bogus Slick. You were supposed to be my friend but you're sleeping with my wife. How do you think I feel?"

"I'm not about to go through this with you especially not here in this hospital. Now we can take this outside and I can beat your ass. You've been asking for it and I've been sparing you."

"Sparing me? Yeah you're funny."

He looks at me real nasty before walking back out of the room. I was to the point where I wanted to just shoot him in his shit and be done with it.

She ends up sleeping the whole day with her parents and I taking turns sitting with her.

***

It was Saturday afternoon and I take a break from sitting with Shy at the hospital to go kick it with my mother and my sisters. I take them out to eat at a Hibachi steak house. Although my mom could be a handful at times, she was all I had.

"So was that your new car?" she questions as we take our seats in the restaurant.

"Na, it's a rental. I wrecked my truck on yesterday."

"And you didn't have the decency to call and tell me. Are you ok?"

"Yes I'm ok."

"What happened? Were you by yourself?"

"Na I was with my girl. She's still in the hospital right now. She got pinned in the truck. They had to cut her out after it flipped several times."

"Damn. I pray she's ok. I don't wish the pain of losing a child on anyone. I'm glad you're ok too son. You know I would lose my mind if anything ever happened to you. You're my first born and my only son."

I look at her and start to cry.

"What's wrong?"

"What if she doesn't wake up Ma?"

"What have I always told you as a child? Have faith in God that he will make everything ok. She's going to be fine."

I use the napkin to wipe my face.

"I really have to meet this girl that has you crying and all in your feelings."

"She got my brother open like a can of worms," Saniyah says.

"You just better not let me find out about a nigga having you open like a can of worms or I'm beating some ass," I respond throwing a napkin at her.

"They know better. Ain't no boyfriends until they are at least 16. I'm not ready to be no grand mama."

"Well you better get ready cause I want to have some kids."

"At least get married first."

"Married or not, I still want to be a father. I'm ready to do for my kids what my father never got to do for me."

"In due time God will bless you with a child of your own. Just trust his timing. Don't be in such a rush. You don't want to go out here and have a child by someone that's going to make your life a living hell for 18 plus years. Thank God you don't have any by Chanel. Her ass wouldn't know how to change a diaper or fix a bottle."

"I never did like her Slick."

"So what have yall girls been doing this Summer?"

"Staying at the mall and the skating rink," my mom answers.

"Imma pop up at the skating rink one Saturday night to see what the hell yall be down there doing."

"Don't be trying to embarrass us Slick."

"I'm not gone embarrass yall. Everybody loves me."

"When everything gets better with your girlfriend I would like to meet her."

"That can be arranged. I'll cook a big dinner and have you guys over the house."

"Hell yeah. About time you cook for your mama."

"Don't you start. You know I always use to cook before I moved out."

"You moved out at 19 and you're now 25. Do the math. That doesn't even count anymore."

"It has not been that long. You be flexing Ma."

***

I arrive at the hospital and see that Shy was sitting up in bed while her mom held a pitcher of water to her mouth. Her eyes light up once she sees me.

"Hey beautiful. How are you feeling?"

I sit on the edge of the bed and kiss her on the cheek.

"I feel ugly."

"You're so beautiful. Don't say that."

"She's been wanting a mirror for the past hour," her mom says.

"You don't need a mirror when you have me baby. How are you feeling?"

"I can't move my leg."

"It's broken babe."

"How am I going to get around?"

"We will get you a wheelchair now quit worrying."

After Shy's mom leaves, I sit up in the bed next to her and we watch *A Thin Line Between Love and Hate* on USA. The dietary staff brings her up a tray for dinner. I feed her and wash her face and hands once she's done eating.

"I appreciate you babe for being here."

"I told you I was gone always be here for you."

"I thought something had happened to you. I just knew God didn't give me something great just to take it away like that," she tells me.

"I am just fine. We just gotta focus on getting you back walking again."

She lays her head on my chest.

"I just wanna be back in home in bed with you and Mason."

"Don't even think about that right now. You will be back home in due time."

Her pain medicine starts dripping into her IV and I could tell she was getting sleepy. She starts yawning and rubbing her eyes.

"Slick."

"Yes baby."

"I'm going to have all of your babies."

"Oh really."

"Yes all six of them."

"Six?"

"Umm hmmm Slick Jr. Slick the 3rd. Slikesha."

She starts snoring. She was sound asleep on my chest. I rub my hand up and down her back while admiring how beautiful she was. I kiss her on the forehead before continuing to watch the movie.

Slick

It was the start of a new work week and the only thing on my mind was getting through today so I could go back up to the hospital with Shy.

I was on break sitting at the table with my boys while snacking on a bag of chips and drinking a Coke.

"It's a damn shame I gotta look on the news to find out my best friend had a bad wreck."

"Shit has been so hectic man, but I apologize. You know I would've called and told you."

"How is Shy doing?"

"She is awake without the feeding tube so she can now talk and stuff. Her face is swollen and bruised from the airbag and her left leg is broken. She has to wear a cask, but other than that baby girl is good. They just holding her now to make sure all her tests come back good before they release her."

"I saw your truck and almost didn't recognize it. Where was yall headed anyway?"

"To the airport to catch a flight to Florida for the weekend."

"Shit, I'm trying to travel like yall. Damn you just got

back from Vegas."

"You're so sprung. Nigga it's written all over your face. Her pussy must be magical."

"It tastes like it."

We all erupt with laughter.

"So have you and Ashanti decided on a wedding date?"

"Next year on the last weekend in August."

"Have you decided on a location?"

"Now that we are undecided on, but we got a couple of venues in mind."

"I'm just ready for the bachelor's party. You already know I'm cutting up."

"Don't cut up too bad. I'd hate for Desiree to kill you the next day."

"Let's go to Los Angeles for the bachelor's party or New Orleans. I'm trying to do something big."

"How big are we talking? You and I are on two different budgets. I have three kids and you have none."

"That's why you get a travel agent and book early as possible for great discounts."

"Sounds like a plan, but no women allowed. Slick don't you try and sneak Shy to California now."

"Fuck you Rob."

"We gone arrive in California and Shy gone already be waiting at the hotel. You know you act like you can't go a day without her."

"Don't be a hater all your life nigga."

"Let me ask you a question Slick. As a man with no kids of his own, you don't have a problem with dating a woman with a child."

"Not at all. I just consider the fact that she has a child as a bonus. Now I got two people to care for and spend time with."

"You're a good man bro. Glad you found someone that can bring out the best in you," Jaylen announces.

"Chanel was draining you."

"Chanel still is draining me. She keeps popping up saying she's pregnant. The bitch is delusional."

"How long ago did yall break up and she's still popping up?"

"Hell yeah that's the reason we were late to the river boat. We get outside and she sitting on the hood of my truck."

"What you be doing to these women bruh?"

"Being a good man. She know she fucked up that's all that is. She just miss this money train. Her ass aint trying to do nothing with her life."

"Like most of these women around here."

"I gotta go by the lot and check on the house and see how much progress they done made."

"Your house warming party gone be super lit. Ashanti gone be my designated driver because I'm getting wasted. If she says no then I'll just crash on the couch."

"Sounds like a plan. I'm cool with that."

"Mase ass just keeps looking over here."

"The way I'm feeling today he better just keep looking."

"Slick aka Mr. Steal Ya Girl."

"Na I just know to treat a woman how I would want a man to treat my mom or my sisters."

The rest of my work day went by smooth. Once the clock struck four, I clock out and race back to the hospital to see how Shy was doing.

When I arrive at the hospital Shy was no longer in her

room. I walk to the nurse's station to see where they had moved her too. Her mother and father were walking out of the waiting area with a look of sadness written all over their faces.

"Where is Shy?"

"We've been trying to call you Slick."

"What happened? She was just doing fine."

"They had to rush her back for another surgery. She had a seizure out of nowhere and they found bleeding on her brain."

I walk up and down the hall trying not to let my emotions get the best of me. I just know God was not about to take her away from me like this.

After what seems like forever, the doctor walks out of the OR with a frantic and apologetic look on his face.

"NOOO NOOO NOOO!" I hear her mom say as she starts crying.

I walk out of the hospital. I sit in the parking lot in the rental car crying like a little boy. It had even started to rain. The rain drops fell hard against the roof of the car. I haven't felt a pain like this since my father had passed away. There was no words to describe it.

I hear a knock on my passenger's side window. I press the unlock button and Derrick slides into the car.

"I can't stay here another minute. Let's go have some drinks, my treat. You might need it more than me anyway."

I pull myself together before her father and I head to The Pizza Spot. It was a hookah lounge and bar about ten minutes from the hospital. We get a table at the back of the restaurant and he tells the waiter to start a tab. I knew right then that tonight was going to be a long night for the both of us.

After downing five shots back to back, he was starting to get emotional.

"You know I still remember Shy's first day of kindergarten. She had on a pink shirt with some blue jean overalls. Her mom sent her to school with a head full of hair bows. Her and Larissa both cried when it was time for her to go into the classroom. She was our miracle baby. After suffering three miscarriages, it seemed like our dream of starting a family was impossible. Until we welcomed a beautiful brown eyed eight pound and 5 ounce baby girl. She was our life sized doll. Larissa kept her dressed like she was an actual doll. She made me a better man and a better husband. I finally found purpose and that was to be a great father."

"And you're doing a damn good job."

He breaks down into tears.

"What if I have to bury my only child?"

"That's not going to happen. She's going to wake up from her coma. Don't think like that."

This was the first time I have seen a grown man cry and it was the most saddest thing I had ever experienced.

***

It was a little after midnight when I finally pull up in front of his house. By the time I got him out of the car and up the front steps, Larissa had already opened the door for us. I could tell she had been crying herself.

"I blew up the air mattress in the den for him. Just take him in there."

"Ok."

"Lord, please don't take my only child," he whines.

"It's going to be ok Derrick. We have to be strong for our grandson right now."

I sit him on the air mattress and he falls back. She takes off his shoes and throws a blanket over him.

"Thank you for making sure he made it home safely. You're a good man Slick."

"It's no problem at all. Have you gotten any sleep?"

"Nope. When I'm not crying. Mason is crying. And when he's not crying, I'm crying. It's just been a stressful day for everyone."

"Yeah it really has been. I just feel so numb right now. I don't know what to do right now."

"None of us do. We just have to pray that she pulls through this. The last time Derrick got drunk like this was when he found out she had gotten married."

"I would've been crying if my daughter had married a fool too."

She laughs a little bit.

"You got that right. Well drive safe Slick. I'm going to try and get an hour of sleep while Mason is sleeping."

I slowly drive home with Calvin Richardson's *Can't Let Go* blasting through the speakers.

I get home, shower, and just lay in bed looking at the ceiling. I needed Shy to pull through this. Life just wouldn't seem right if she wasn't by my side.

Slick

Hours turned into days and days turned into weeks and Shy was still in a comatose state. To get me out of my depressed apartment, the boys invite me out to some event that was being held at the strip club downtown. It's been a long time since I actually been out on the club scene and this is probably what I needed.

We were all chilling in the back of the club sitting around a circular table. I had ordered me a bottle of E & J from the bar while Jaylen and Rob were sipping on white.

"It's some bad bitches up in here tonight," announces Rob.

"Surprised Desiree let you out the house."

"I wear the pants in my relationship."

"Shittt since when?"

"Fuck you Jay."

"Yall just behave. I don't need yall girls calling me tomorrow asking what happened."

"Well Ashanti already told me I can have as much as fun as I want. She knows I'm not going to do anything to jeopardize us getting married."

My bottle arrives and I take it to the head.

"So glad you're not the one driving tonight."

"Let him drink as much as he want. After all you've been through, you deserve a night out to enjoy yourself and to get back in the swing of things. You know I'm going to make sure you get home safely," Jaylen responds.

"Well I'm going to see some ass shaking. I'll get up with yall later."

Rob takes the rest of his cup to the head before getting up and walking in the direction of the stage.

Jaylen soon gets up and walks off to get a private dance from some big booty stripper. I sit at the table and just watch the ladies from afar while nursing my half empty bottle.

A beautiful brown skinned beauty that was rocking a yellow G-string and bra comes over to me. I can't lie she was sexy as shit, but I didn't feel right having fun while Shy was laying up in a hospital bed.

She turns my chair around and straddles my lap.

"Hey handsome."

"I'm not interested in a lap dance."

"Well according to your friend at the bar you need something to uplift your spirits. Plus he already paid for it."

"Well you can keep the money lil mama I'm good."

"You're so handsome. I wonder what all things I can do to you in the private room," she says as she kisses on my neck.

She starts rubbing her hands through my waves and then tries to kiss me. I turn my head and look towards the bar. I see Mase sitting there waving.

"I don't mean to be rude, but you have to get up. I shouldn't even be here."

I push her up off me, but not hard enough to make her fall. By the time I make my way to the bar, Mase wasn't anywhere around.

I tell the boys I'm leaving and that I wasn't feeling it. I end up catching a Lyft back to my apartment. I didn't even make it to the bed. I crash in the den on the couch.

***

The next morning I was up at the hospital with Shy bright and early. I was sitting at the foot of the hospital bed massaging her feet with some Peppermint smelling foot rub. I was going to paint her nails as well. I know she'd have a fit if she saw the way her nail polished was chipped.

This had become my daily routine. I would bring her fresh flowers, massage her feet, and sing her a song in hopes that she'd hear my voice and wake up.

"You fix your make up, just so. Guess you don't know, that your beautiful. Try on every dress that you own. You were as fine in my eyes, a half hour ago. If your mirror won't make it any clearer I'll be the one to let you know Out of all of the girls you're my one and only girl. Ain't nobody in world tonight. All of the stars, you make them shine like they were ours ain't nobody in the world but you and I. You and I. Ain't nobody in the world but you....."

I look up at her and smile.

"You do know that if you don't wake up, I'll have to find another girlfriend and I'm pretty certain that you wouldn't want another girl kissing all on me. I'm pretty sure you wouldn't want another girl giving me those six kids your promised me."

"And then we still have to move into the house and decorate. I'm not really one for interior decorating so yeah you need to wake up babe."

"Mason needs you baby. I need you. No one would be able to be as good a mother as you. I know you don't want Mase getting remarried and having some ratchet girl raising your child. That's a negative."

"By the way Jaylen's bachelor party is being held in Cali. If you want me to sneak you out there in my luggage, you have to pull through. Our love story is just getting started. I don't want it to be over so soon. I have dreams of making you my wife and us having a destination wedding in

Africa."

I kiss her on the hand.

"I love you Shy and I need you to get better for me."

***

Every morning before I leave for work, I wipe her down with some warm soapy water. I wash her face and comb her hair while singing to her. Every night before I lay down on the air mattress next to her bed, I do the same.

There was no place I'd rather be than right here by her side.

"Good morning baby girl," I say pulling the curtains back and opening the blinds.

I walk in her bathroom to wash my hands. When I walk back out, her doctor and nurse were in the room along with Mase.

"What's going on?"

"We've made the decision to pull the plug."

"Like hell you have."

"I'm her husband so I have the final say. You're just her boyfriend remember that. She is suffering and I'm not about to put her through that any longer. My son doesn't need to see his mother like this."

"She was suffering when she was alive and you didn't give a fuck about that."

"I'm not about to go back and forth with you when I'm the one that makes all of the decisions."

"Have you talked to her parents?"

"I don't have to talk to anybody. Did you not just here what I been saying for the past few minutes?"

"Wait a minute let me call her parents. They at least have the right to say goodbye to their only child you heartless bastard."

I walk out of the room and call Derrick informing him to get to the hospital asap. Once they arrive, Larissa takes some paperwork to the doctor.

"Yall got ample amount of time to say goodbye. I made the decision to pull the plug."

"No you're not pulling the plug. As of today, I was awarded her power of attorney due to the status of your marriage by the mayor."

"What status?" he questions.

"Yall are separated waiting on the annulment to be finalized."

"So I guess since you're the power of attorney, you gone

pay this high ass hospital bill too? Cause she's technically still on my insurance. Let Slick pay the damn bill then."

"LEAVE NOW!" Larissa screams.

Mase took one look at me and then her parents before heading towards the elevators.

We all go back in Shy's room and take a seat around the bed. I grab and squeeze her hand.

"I wish you could see yourself through my eyes to really know how much you mean to me."

***

The next few days were a blur to me. I wasn't really getting much sleep and I was losing hope. I sit beside her bed holding onto her hand.

"You really need to go home and get some rest Slick. You look awful. I know you want to be here when she wakes up, but I'm pretty sure she will understand that you needed some rest. Go home for a night or two and get yourself together."

"I can't go home. My mind starts racing and I can't sleep."

"Your ass gone fall out running off two and three hours of sleep like this."

The doctor walks in.

"Hey how is everyone doing today? Has she been responsive any today?"

"Na."

He lifts up her eyelids and shines a light in both eyes before thumping her on the knees with some plastic tool to see if she would respond, but she didn't.

I grab her hand and kiss it.

"Babe if you can hear me, just move your fingers or blink one time."

Within a few seconds she moved one of her fingers. I lean up and kiss her on the forehead.

"If you can hear me squeeze my hand babe."

Softly, she squeezes my hand. Tears run down my cheeks.

"I love you girl."

"She's responding to your voice. That's a good sign. We've ran some tests on her brain and she may suffer a little memory loss regarding the accident, but everything else seems fine. I'll be back to check in again later."

Before he exits the room, he stops and turns to face us.

"There is also one more thing you should know. We see

that she's pregnant."

Shy

I was lying in a hospital bed with a feeding tube down my throat unable to speak. My eyes wander over and I see Slick sitting in a chair beside the bed watching television. He had his hand on the bed so I move my hand over to his and grab it. I guess I scared him because he jumps up and looks at me. His eyes grew big once he saw that I was staring at him. He bombard me with kisses all over my face.

"I'm going to get the nurse. I'll be right back babe. Don't move."

It's not like I could move anyway, but ok. He runs out of the room and I hear him calling for a nurse.

They come in the room and sits me up in the bed and takes the feeding tube out of my mouth. She then hands me a pitcher of water and tells me to drink something.

"Do you know where you are?" she asks.

I shake my head yes.

"I'm going to contact your doctor. I'll be back shortly."

She leaves and Slick sits on the bed next to me. He kisses me on the forehead. He grabs my hand and intertwines his fingers with mine.

"I'm just so happy that you're awake baby. It's so much

I have to tell you."

"Like what?" I say in a voice barely above a whisper.

The feeding tube had my throat sore so I wasn't trying to talk for real.

"You're pregnant."

I look up at him.

"Don't look at me like that. It's your fault. You always tryna hunch on me."

I try not to laugh as I lay my head on his chest.

"I love you Shy."

"I love you too."

"Everybody's talking about heaven like they just can't wait to go. Saying how it's gonna be so good, so beautiful. Lying next to you, in this bed with you, I aint convinced. Cause, I don't know how, I don't know how heaven, heaven could be better than this," he sings.

***

It was my first day back at home. Slick carries me upstairs to my room and sits me on the edge of the bed. He helps me get changed into something more comfortable.
"Do you need anything babe?"

"Yes, a kiss."

He sits beside me and we share a kiss.

"Don't tease me. You know I haven't had sex in a little over a month."

"I got a surprise for you."

"What?"

"Hand me my hospital bag and close your eyes."

He grabs my bag from the hospital and sits back down beside me. I watch him close his eyes before pulling the ultrasound out.

"Here you go babe. I took these yesterday when you went home to shower and change clothes."

He starts getting teary eyed.

"Babe don't cry."

He leans over and kisses me again.

"You've made me so happy babe. I got to frame this. I'm about to be a father."

"What if it's another boy?"

"We will just have two big headed boys running around."

"I was not expecting this at all."

"Me either, but I'm excited. We gotta hurry up and get you started with physical theraphy so you can be walking again in no time. I hope you're walking again before Thanksgiving."

"Me too. I'm not trying to be in this wheelchair the remainder of the year. That'll suck."

"The fellas have been asking about you and the ladies sent you a gift."

"I gotta call and tell them thank you. Too bad I don't have a cell phone anymore."

"That's a good thing. We can start fresh. Both of us getting brand new phones and new numbers."

"Great cause Samsung Galaxy has a new phone out and so does iPhone. I saw the commercials in the hospital."

He pulls me close to him.

"Thank you for coming into my life when you did Shy. I'm so much better because of you."

***

I was sitting up in bed holding a squirming Mason. He had gotten so big since the last time I held him and he had a head full of soft curls. Ma walks in the room just as I was holding him in the air while biting his toes. He was giggling and slobbering out the mouth.

"Look at his juicy self. He's so chubby now."

"Don't be talking about my fat man. Aint that right Mason?"

I lay him on my chest and give him his pacifier. Ma takes a seat on the bed.

"How are you feeling?"

"Tired."

"Girl you been sleep forever I know you lying."

I start laughing.

"I'm serious. My body feels like it just wants to lay down."

"We have to get you in physical therapy asap because the more you sit around idle, the more tired you will be."

"I appreciate you for not letting Mase pull the plug on me."

"Girl you know damn well that was not about to happen. Your grandfather was not having that. By the way you need to call him. He's been asking about you nonstop. Him and Ma even came by the hospital a couple of times to sit with you."

"I'll call him soon."

"I can't believe you're pregnant again. I told you that you were going to have me another grandbaby."

"I wasn't expecting to be pregnant this damn soon. I look crazy pregnant and my son is not even six months yet."

"Girl fuck what people think. You got one life to live. If you are happy so the fuck what. You could've been six feet under, but you're not and I still get to see your beautiful face every day. If anybody has something negative to say, tell them to kiss your ass or come talk to me."

"I most certainly will."

"I'm just happy I get to go through the different stages of your pregnancy this time. I'm doing a gender reveal, a pamper shower, a baby shower, a sip and see, all of it."

"A sip and see?"

"Yes we can sip wine while everyone admire how beautiful my grandbaby is while lying in their swing."

"My God."

"You just get ready because I am going to be so extra. Don't let it be a girl. I'm going to have her at the spa with me while Mason is out fishing with his PawPaw."

"What yall cooked? I want something sweet like a

cheese cake or a pecan pie."

"You want too much now."

"Did Slick ever come back?"

"Girl he never left. He downstairs drinking beer and watching TV with your father. They been so close these past few weeks. You would think Slick was his son."

"Tell Slick he needs to come on upstairs. He not about to be spending more time with my dad than me."

"Stop hating."

She grabs Mason off my chest and leaves out of the room.

"Quit taking my child Ma."

"Hush. I'm your mama."

I hear her going downstairs. Slick returns to the room a few minutes later.

"What's up babe?" he says giving me a kiss.

"I want to spend some time with you."

"You know I have nothing but time for my honey."

"What you and my daddy were talking about?"

"We doing a father and son weekend in Vegas. He say he's never been so I want to show him a good time."

"My mama is not letting my dad go to no Vegas."

"She already said he could go since it's with me. Don't you get jealous cause your father likes me now."

"Whatever."

"Don't be trying to give me hell with your pregnancy mood swings."

"Are you spending the night with me?"

"Of course. It's your first night back at home. You know I wasn't going to not stay with you."

He gets up and locks the room door before coming back to the bed. He lifts up my night gown and spread my legs apart. He kisses from my breasts down to my clit while keeping eye contact with me.

"I've been missing this," he tells me.

He bites and sucks on my lips making me lose my mind.

Slick

After I get off work, I pull up to Shy parents' house. I had plans on taking her to the park so she could get out of the house and enjoy some sunlight. I also wanted to ride by the house and see how much work they had gotten done in these past few weeks.

When I pull up, I see two additional cars in the driveway so I park on the curb. Before I could even make it up the steps I hear yelling coming from inside. The front door was open, but the screen door was closed so I let myself in.

I see a man who I knew to be the Mayor from watching all of his TV campaigns, who I assumed to be his wife, and Shy's aunt Lorraine along with Derrick and Larissa in the den.

"Well hello everyone."

"Have a seat Slick," Derrick tells me.

"What's going on?"

"This bitch let her daughter try and kill yall. That's what happened."

Larissa was waving the pictures from the traffic cameras around in the air.

"It's her tag on the pictures Lorraine. I don't care how

you try and make the shit look sweet, it's your fuckin child. My baby was in a coma, damn near dead for a fuckin month and you're sitting here trying to justify the bullshit. No wonder yall asses didn't come to the hospital not once. Your ass knew."

"I wouldn't want my own niece to die. You sound stupid Larissa. I would never want to hurt my own damn niece."

"So where is your child and when are you going to turn her into the police?"

"Terrica is a grown ass woman and I can't get ahold of her."

"Cause you not trying too. If Daddy wasn't sitting here, I'd jump across this couch and beat your ass."

"Hey. I need both of yall to calm down. How did yall even let it get this far?" the mayor was speaking in a calm tone.

"Daddy, I'm not letting this go. That's my baby up there in a wheelchair all because of Terrica's stupid ass. Mad over a fuckin man that's still married to her damn cousin. If the dick makes you turn on your own damn family, I don't want it."

"Lorraine, you have 24 hours to turn Terrica into the police or they will be issuing a warrant. A hit and run is a felony all by itself."

"Daddy, can't you do something? That's your

granddaughter we're talking about."

"Hell na he can't do nothing. Bitch he got a grand daughter upstairs in a wheelchair right now. Right is right and wrong is wrong."

"What the fuck ever Larissa. You always have been Daddy's favorite. If it was Shy, he'd be breaking his back to keep her ass outta jail."

"You truly are stupid. Your daughter is a criminal. Now go find her ass so you can take her to the police station. When it comes to my child, I'll go against anybody. Family included. You wasn't thinking about family when you were trying to murder my damn baby. If she would've died and left her son motherless, I wouldn't be able to get you heifers to buy a can a milk or offer to babysit."

"Whatever I'm out. I see how it is. Yall always have made me and my child feel like outcasts. Always kissing Larissa and Derrick's ass. Fuck this family."

She gets up and storms out of the house slamming the door along the way. Larissa jumps off the couch and runs after her. Derrick catches her before she could go outside.

"You might as well gone head upstairs."

"But Derrick."

"And you wonder where Shy gets her temper from."

"Just let me hit her one time. Pleaseeeee babe."

"I'm not gone let you fight your sister."

"But her daughter could've killed our child," she cries.

"Calm down. Go upstairs and check on Shy and Mason."

"I just want to beat her ass one good time babe. She is not about to keep disrespecting me after all I done did for her and her ungrateful ass daughter."

"I know Rissa. We got enough going on right now. We don't need to give DHR any more reasons to pop up for a home welfare check."

"Listen to your husband, Rissa. I know you're upset about Shy, but I told yall to break her up from dating that Mase guy years ago. It's both of yall fault. Now look at all the bullshit that's going on. I'm trying to get reelected as Mayor. I don't need my family making headline news. You know how your mama is. YALL RUNNING HER DAMN BLOOD PRESSURE UP! Imma go do some damage control so we can keep this away from the media. In the meantime, Larissa quit harassing your sister."

"Dad, did you not just hear how she talked to me?"

"You have bigger things to worry about like Shy being pregnant again."

"What the hell is that supposed to mean?"

"Nothing at all, but I have some important papers for her

so go take these upstairs," he says handing Larissa a manila envelope.

"I'll go take it to her. I need to be checking on her anyway."

"I'm sorry son. I didn't get to catch your name."

"I'm Solomon, but everyone calls me Slick."

"Well I'm Ralph and this is my wife Shirley."

I get up and shake their hands as I'm headed up the stairs.

"Oh Slick, Shy got some envelope in the mail today. Take that upstairs too."

Larissa hands me an envelope that was on the end table by the front door.

"Next time you, me, and Derrick have got to get together for drinks or think about joining us on our fishing trips on the weekends."

"Shy will have a fit if you have him gone from sun up to sun down like you do with Derrick."

"Ah she'll get over it. I got a bond with my son-in-law and my future grandson-in-law."

I laugh before heading upstairs.

I open the door to Shy's room and see that she is sound asleep with Mason lying next to her kicking and squirming around. I sit on the bed and pick him up.

"Hey lil man. How was your day?"

He starts kicking and slobbering at the mouth.

"Tell your mama it's time to get up."

I put him to her face and let him try and give her kisses. She wakes up and sees me.

"Damn how long was I asleep?"

"I don't know, but you better not fall asleep on my baby no more."

"Oh you hush."

"You got some mail too."

I hand her the envelopes. I scoot up in the bed next to her and talk to Mason.

"Damn man you already teething."

"They say when babies start developing fast that they are moving out the way for another one," Shy tells me.

"I guess my soldiers march after all."

"Yeah whatever. BABE GUESS WHAT?"

"What?"

"I GOT MY ANULMEMT PAPERS!"

"You excited aint ya?"

"HELL THE FUCK YEAH! I'm framing these hoes."

"Well I gotta go pee. Imma put lil man in his swinger."

"Ok."

I sit Mason in his swing before walking into her adjacent bathroom. I couldn't even finish urinating before I hear Shy calling my name. I walk back in the room and she is looking at a picture.

"Slick, please tell me you weren't with another girl when I was in the hospital."

"No, I wasn't. What type of man do you think I am?"

"Then what is this?"

She throws the picture on the bed and I pick it up. It was an image of me at the strip club when the stripper was trying to give me a lap dance.

"Yall look pretty damn close to me. Hell in fact she's on your lap kissing your damn neck. And then there's a note attached *You thought you were going to find better, but ended up with the same type of nigga. Jokes on you. Ha ha ha."*

"Babe you have got to believe me. I know what it looks like, but I promise nothing happened."

"Oh really? I can't damn tell."

"Shy, please don't get upset."

"You knew the shit I went through in my marriage and you're at a fuckin club while I was in the hospital with some bitch."

She starts crying in her hands. I pull her hands off her face.

"Look at me. I promise you baby nothing happened. Just hear me out first please."

"WHAT SLICK! WHAT IS THERE TO HEAR?"

"I didn't do anything. Jaylen and Rob left the table to go watch the strippers on stage and I stayed at the table. I had me a bottle so I was drinking and chilling. Next thing I know a bitch walk up, straddles my lap, and says hey your friend at the bar paid for you a lap dance. I look up to see Mase stupid ass waving and grinning. By the time I got her off my lap and got to the bar, he had dipped. You know me better than that Shy for you to think I would be with some girl while you're in the hospital fighting for your life. I think I deserve some type of credit. Have I given you any reason thus far to think that I would cheat on you?"

"No."

"You're going to let Mase, the man who didn't care enough about you to not sleep with your family member, cause you to lose out on happiness and a dose of real love."

I lean over and give her a kiss.

"You love me?"

"Of course I do."

"Good cause I love you too. That's all that matters right now. You don't need to be up under any type of stress while you're pregnant with my seed."

"Yes Dr. Slick."

"I think we should do a big cook out to celebrate everything good that is happening in our lives. You're no longer married, you're pregnant, and most important you made it out of the hospital in good health."

"Are you going to invite your mother?"

"Of course. It's time you met her and my sisters. You are going to be the mother of her first grandchild you know."

"I just hope she likes me babe."

"What's not to like about you?"

"You're absolutely right. I'm the queen."

"You gah damn right."

We both laugh together before I pull her into a hug.

"I'm rocking with you and only you. Never let anyone tell you otherwise especially not Mase's punk ass."

"You're right."

I kiss her on the forehead.

Slick

After driving around in a rental for the past month, the insurance company finally cut me a check for totaling out my truck. I was now at the dealership with my mama picking out a new vehicle. We were walking the lot looking at the newer model SUVs.

"So how has everything been?"

"Stressful, but I'm making it. Having a house built is stressful all by itself and then the accident happened. It's just been crazy and now Shy is pregnant."

She stops walking.

"PREGNANT?"

"Yes we found out while she was still in the hospital."

"Really Slick?"

"What. I thought you'd be happy I mean it is your first grandchild."

"You barely even know this girl. What if yall don't work out and she hits your ass with child support? They gone try and take everything you got."

"Why do you have to think of all the things that could go wrong instead of being happy and enjoying the moment?"

"Whatever Slick. I'm just saying."

"See this is why I don't tell you nothing. You're never really happy for me. You try and rain on my parade every chance you get."

"Slick I am your mother. I will never feel bad for voicing my opinion. You came out my coochie. Don't forget that."

"Yeah whatever. You like this one?" I ask pointing to a black three row seater Suburban.

"Why you like these big old trucks and SUVS?"

"Because I'm a man. What I look like driving around in a Honda or an Impala? I need room and space for two kids."

"Two kids? She's having twins?"

"No, she already has a son."

"What the hell have you gotten yourself into? Don't you think you're moving too fast? Does she even work?"

"She's in a wheelchair. How in the hell is she going to work right now with a broken leg? Where is all of this built up animosity coming from? You were so excited to meet her when she was in the hospital?"

"Yeah before I knew she was damn pregnant and already had a child. Why the hell would you want to raise another man's baby?"

"The same reason the twins dad got with you when you were a single parent raising me."

"Hey, I'm just trying to look out for you. I just don't want her to end up doing you like Chanel did you."

"Don't ever compare Shy to Chanel. They are not the same. Hell they not even similar."

"Ok."

"I think I like this Denali better than the Suburban."

"Can you even afford this?"

"Please don't start counting my pockets. I can afford whatever I decide to purchase."

"Well excuse me then."

"I'm throwing a barbecue at Shy parents' house this weekend to celebrate her pregnancy and her getting out of the hospital so I hope to see you there."

"Just send me the address and I'll be there. The twins will be at their friends house for a sleepover on Saturday."

"They aint never at home."

"Yes they are."

"When? Every time we talk, the twins are gone somewhere."

"I know that's a lie cause we barely even talk. You get a girlfriend and forget that you even have a mama."

"I damn sho don't forget you on the 1st of the month when all your bills are due so you can kill that."

I swear my mom was a handful at times. Let me stop lying, she was a handful all of the damn time. My only concern right now was Shy, Mason, and our unborn child. What anyone thought about our relationship was irrelevant. I was done taking relationship advice from people that weren't even in a relationship. That's like telling the blind to lead the blind.

I end up cashing out on a Dark gray 2018 Denali XL with a touch screen radio, GPS, and back up camera. When leaving the dealership, my mom goes her way and I drive in the direction of my apartment.

Shy

I was lying in bed with Slick with my cask propped up on some pillows while we watched *Mr. and Mrs Smith* together. While he was all into the movie, I was just admiring how handsome he was. I could not stop smiling. Everything about this man was perfect, from the waves in his head down to his toes. I never thought I would find love again after Mase, but I'm glad I decided to give him a chance.

I can't lie at first I really didn't want to be pregnant again so soon, but I know everything happens for a reason. Plus, I couldn't blame no one but myself. Slick and I had been having sex a whole lot and half of the time I didn't know if we were using protection or not.

I snap out of my thoughts when I feel Slick looking at me.

"What babe?" I question.

"That's what I wanna know. You just be staring at me hard as fuck."

"Cause I love you and you make me so happy."

"I love you too."

"I can't wait to get out of this cask. I can't even get freaky like I want too."

"You're such a freak."

"Only for you nigga."

"Better be."

He leans over and kisses me and again and again. His kisses taste like honey and I didn't want him to stop. He kisses down to my neck and begins to gently suck and bite on it.

"Babe you know that's my spot."

"Just let me make you feel good."

Before long he had me laying on my stomach on a stack of pillows so I wouldn't put pressure on my broken leg while he was hitting it from the back. He kisses my ear while pulling my hair.

"Tell me you love me."

"I love you babe."

He pulls my head back and kisses me passionately. I feel myself exploding all over his dick.

"I can't believe your pussy gone be this wet for nine months. You gone drive me crazy."

"That's impossible. You're already crazy baby."

"Yeah crazy over you."

***

It was Saturday afternoon. Slick and my parents had decided to throw me a barbecue to celebrate all of the great news that we've been receiving lately. Specifically, my pregnancy. He had invited his home boys and their girlfriends. I would also be meeting his mom for the first time and I just had a funny feeling that she wasn't going to like me.

Slick and my father were at the grocery store getting the beer and liquor while I was in the kitchen not doing a damn thing but watching my mama make the chicken salad.

"I'm nervous," I admit to my mother.

"Nervous for what? You should be happy. You're no longer married to that jackass and you're finally at peace."

"Nervous about meeting Slick's mom for the first time."

"Well she has no choice but to like you or I'll beat her up."

"That's alright Ma. That is not what I had in mind," I say with a laugh.

"Well quit worrying so much .What is there not to love about you?"

"You're right."

Slick and my dad walks in the kitchen carrying cases of beer.

"Now why yall went and bought all this beer?"

"You aint seen nothing. We got more outside."

"That don't make no damn sense. Derrick you know you don't need to be drinking."

"Don't you start that fussing. It's supposed to be a great day. We are celebrating a lot today. My baby is no longer married to that asshole. I'm turning up."

"Oh God," I say.

"Well after yall put the beer up, gone outside and fire up the grill. I already got the meat prepped."

"Yes boss lady."

My dad turns to walk out of the kitchen, but Slick comes over to me.

"You like nice today beautiful."

"Thank You."

He leans down and we share a kiss.

"The fellas and their girls will be here in a few. Ashanti been saying how she is so ready to see you."

"Are they bringing the kids?"

"I don't think so. When I last talked to Jaylen, they were pulling up to Ashanti mom's house."

"Ok then."

"Well let me go bring the rest of this stuff in."

He walks out of the kitchen and I just smile.

"You're in love with that man. It's written all over your face."

"I know it. I wasn't expecting this to happen, but I'm glad it did. He's a great man."

"Your grandfather said the same. He even invited him fishing."

"When did granddad meet him?"

"The other day him and your grandmother had stopped by."

"And they didn't come upstairs and wake me up. That's low down."

"Girl hush. You can see them anytime."

"No I can't. I can't drive."

"Well I'll take you by to see them next week now quit

whining. You sound like a big baby."

"I am a big baby. I'm only 21."

She throws a piece of ham at me

"Heyyyyyy. I'm telling Dad."

"Cry baby."

"Your mama."

"Hey, she's your grandmama. Imma tell her too."

"You better not."

***

Everyone was outside in the yard chilling. Dad and the fellas were playing Dominoes. I was sitting on Slick's lap leaning back against his chest.

"BUBBLE NIGGA!"

Rob throws down his cross deuce

"NOW RUN ME MY MUTHAFUCKIN MONEY."

The remaining players each put $20 on the table and Rob grabs it. My dad washes the bones and they each pull seven dominoes. Slick leads with the big six.

"Damn man don't you think you need to let your girl

breath?" Rob questions.

"You need to get you some business cause this right here is mine."

"Quit being a sucker. You making us men look bad."

"Oh trust me you make look bad even without my help."

"Don't touch that," Derrick says while throwing out a six five.

"Thank you for doing that. You just helped me out. Now touch that nigga," Jaylen responds.

Slick kisses me on the cheek.

"What you thinking about?" he whispers in my ear.

"You."

His phone vibrates in his pocket.

"Babe pull my phone out my pocket. I think it's my mom calling."

I pull his phone out and put it to his ear.

"Hello… Yeah you're at the right house. I'm about to walk around to the front right now."

Slick picks me up and sits me back in my wheelchair before going around to the front of the house. While he was away, Jaylen and Derrick get up to go grab another beer. While the table was clear, my mom comes and sits on my dad's lap. They share a kiss.

"EWWW!"

"Girl don't act like that. How you think you got here?"

"Trust me I don't want to see that visual in my head Ma."

Slick returns to the backyard followed by a middle aged woman who reminded me of Lynn from Girlfriends. She walks up to the table and Slick introduces us.

"Hey you guys this is my mother Cynthia. Ma this is Shy and her parents Derrick and Larissa."

"It's nice to meet you," my mom says extending her hand.

Cynthia eyes were stuck on my dad. She didn't even bother shaking my mom's hand.

"This is the girl you're dating Slick?"

"Hold up what the hell are you trying to say?" my mom asks getting all defensive.

"So you're going to act like you don't remember me Derrick?"

"Should I?"

"Yeah 26 years ago, you gave me money for an abortion remember?"

My mom gets up off my dad's lap.

"Ma you never told me you had an abortion."

"Because I didn't."

My eyes grow big.

"Hold the fuck up. What are you trying to say?"

"I'm not trying to say anything because I'm saying it. Slick is your damn son, Derrick."

I lean over and throw up everywhere.

I WAS PREGNANT BY MY OWN DAMN BROTHER!

Rae Bae

ABOUT THE AUTHOR

Rae Bae, a 27 year old, was born and raised in a small town in Alabama. Other than being an author to a few self-published books, she is also the mother of two beautiful daughters. Her favorite author is James Patterson and biggest inspiration is Tyler Perry. Other than writing, she loves online shopping.

For all book inquiries:

FB: @QueenRaeBae
IG: @Queenrae_bae
SnapChat & Twitter: @Queen_RaeBae

Subscribe to my mailing list at
www.WeLuvRaeBae.com to receive updates on new
book releases, promotions, and more.

Other books by this author:
Late Night Pleasure
Father, I have Sinned
Father, I have Sinned Again
Dangerous Seduction

All books are available on Amazon Kindle and on
paperback.

CPSIA information can be obtained
at www.ICGtesting.com
Printed in the USA
LVHW041821040319
609437LV00001B/128/P

9 781729 135716